Advance praise for *The New Me*

"*The New Me* by Mary Marcus is a revelation. Like Joan Didion she brings to life the nuance and emotion of a sometimes-dysfunctional family life in Southern California with a jaundiced view of Hollywood in her peripheral vision. Like Williams Carlos Williams she knows that precise observation of details can illuminate great depth. Part baby-boom prose poem, part woman's re-birth, *The New Me* is alternately hilarious and heartbreaking and ultimately hopeful. What a cool first novel!"
– Danny Goldberg, author of *Bumping Into Geniuses*

"*The New Me* is funny, poignant and deftly written. It is a relatable story that beats with a pulse of a modern marriage paradigm and provides cringe-worthy moments that simultaneously delight and distress. This book made me uncomfortable in all the best ways. I couldn't put it down."
– Moira Walley-Beckett, Writer/Co-Executive Producer of *Breaking Bad*

"So you think it's all sun, surf and smiles. Mary Marcus shows you the dark side of the California dream. A sadly eloquent, painfully honest account of how a mystery woman intrudes on

a marriage growing melancholy. Reader beware: you might find yourself in these pages."
– Heywood Gould, author of *Cocktail, Fort Apache The Bronx, Greenlight For Murder*

"Mary Marcus expertly illuminates the world of a lived marriage in this inspired novel. With careful nuance and dark humor in her back pocket, she raises questions women might not dare ask themselves. *The New Me* will give the old you something to think about. A real treat."
– Rachel Eddey, author of *Running of the Bride*

"Mary Marcus has created Healthy Harriet and her world with a sharp eye and robust humor. A great debut book parsing the complexities of love, married life, motherhood, and betrayal."
– Alissa Torres, author of *American Widow*

"In *The New Me*, Mary Marcus tells a clever and engaging tale of the intertwined lives of trans-planted modern city-dwellers, which not only illuminates surprising dimensions of our all-too-human strengths and frailties but how the path to self-discovery is seldom what we expect."
– Bran Ferren, Founder, Chief Creative Officer, Applied Minds, LLC

"Have you ever worried you could be replaced by another woman? Have you ever secretly hoped that you might be? Is eighteen years of making dinner every night enough already? These questions haunt the irresistible chef/ wife/mother Harriet Prince in Mary Marcus's funny, heartbreaking and thriller-paced novel, *The New Me*. Marcus serves up the humor and sadness in a threatened empty-nest marriage and reminds us that for even the best cook, end- ings can be bittersweet."

– Delphine Hirsh, author of *The Girls' Guide to Surviving a Breakup*

The New Me

The New Me

Mary Marcus

The Story Plant

Stamford, Connecticut

The Story Plant
Studio Digital CT, LLC
P.O. Box 4331
Stamford, CT 06907

Copyright © 2013 by Mary Marcus
Jacket design by Barbara Aronica Buck

Print ISBN-13: 978-1-61188-138-7
E-book ISBN: 978-1-61188-139-4

"This is Just to Say" By William Carlos Williams, from THE COLLECTED POEMS: VOLUME I, 1909-1939, copyright ©1938 by New Directions Publishing Corp. Reprinted by permission of New Directions Publishing Corp and Carcanet Press Limited.

Visit our website at www.TheStoryPlant.com

First Story Plant Printing: May 2014
Printed in the United States of America
0 9 8 7 6 5 4 3 2 1

To Joel and Amos: for everything

Acknowlegements

I'd like to thank Amos Goodman, Joel Goodman, Lisa Haber, Jason Mayland, Carroll Newman, Jessie Nelson, Jennifer Vincent and Susan Woolhandler—for their time and especially for their talented minds.

I'd also like to express my gratitude to Lou Aronica, my editor and publisher, for his faith and vision.

This Is Just to Say . . .

I have eaten
the plums
that were in
the icebox

and which
you were probably
saving
for breakfast

Forgive me
they were delicious
so sweet
and so cold

William Carlos Williams

PART I

One

LAST NIGHT I WALKED BY MY OLD HOUSE, SOMETHING I've wanted to do for a while now. Since I'm the same old me, driving the same old beat-up Volvo, I parked a few blocks away and set out on foot. I told myself it was just the house I wanted to see, not really them. Next week is Easter and Passover. Days are longer now. When flowers bloom all year long, it's hard to appreciate spring. But spring it is. LA style. The air smelled incredibly sweet.

Everything about my old house looked the same. It's a comfortable Spanish two-story built in the twenties, one that's much nicer inside than out. What's weird is there was not a single potted plant outside the front door. I was counting on pots of daffodils and hyacinths, maybe some kind of spring wreath on the front door. Lights were on in the living room; one of the narrow front windows was cracked open.

When I lived there I used to crack a window to let out the cooking odors, particularly if I was cooking fish. I'm not nearly so fussy in these past months that I've been living alone. My standards were higher with Jules and the boys around. I used to be quite neat. Now days can go by where I don't make the bed; I never would have done that before.

I stood for a bit just taking in the place, feeling apprehensive. What if they saw me? Parked there in the driveway, just like always, was Jules' shiny Beemer with a metal chock wedged up against the back wheel so Jules won't have to go nuts thinking it might roll down the driveway and go crashing into the house across the way. When I was in the kitchen cooking or upstairs late at night, waiting for him to arrive, the sound of the chock scraping across concrete would alert me he was home.

Seeing the Beemer parked there was like seeing Jules himself. Being Jules, he doesn't believe in burglar alarms—according to him, just another thing to break—so I knew it was safe to run my fingers across its shiny white body, so smooth and impeccably clean. Like Jules' body in fact. Touching it gave me a rush. Lydia's car was also on the street—only Jules gets the small driveway—it gave me less of a shock to see her car, perhaps because it's not as familiar. She's still driving her bright blue Mazda with a *Write*

Like A Girl sticker on the back bumper. Its roof was splattered with those berries—we used to call them shitting berries—back when the boys lived there with me, when we were a family. I could never figure out why they didn't fall on Jules' Beemer. Because Lydia is much like I am in certain ways, she probably just nonchalantly brushes them off with a paper towel. Completely opposite of the fit Jules would have if one single berry dared to land on his roof.

As I stood in the dark on the sidewalk, I still must have been in denial. But I inched in a little bit closer, because I was hoping for a glimpse of my cat Pasha. Like housecats everywhere, he spends most of his waking time staring out of windows. And indeed before long I saw a curved form on the window ledge, and in the shadowy gloom, the green glow of Pasha's eyes. He was perched there looking out, taking everything in, but not making a sound. I felt like meowing as I used to and announcing, "Pasha! Pasha it's me, I'm home!" I wondered too, if it was really Pasha, but of course it had to be. I would have heard if he had died.

Pasha is perfectly beautiful with gorgeous markings. When I lived there he was fat. As I stood there in the dark, I forgave him all his catty sins and fervently wished I had taken him with me. By the time I moved out, Jules and Lydia were so eager to be alone and rid of me they would have given me Pasha. It's too late, of course, to get him back. Unless I sneak in there and steal him, which is a thought, but by now Jules must have changed the locks. That would have been the first thing he did once they got me out of the house.

Pasha was never that affectionate but he was my son Dan's cat, then my cat, and if not the flesh of my flesh than certainly the fur of my flesh. If I was away from the house too long, particularly in those last years, I'd think, *I can't keep poor Pasha waiting another minute; he'll miss me too much.* Does Pasha miss me now? Right away he angled in on Lydia, circling her ankles, marking her with his handsome head. She seemed part of us right away.

"Lifeboat material!" Jules proclaimed after the first time she came to our house for dinner. And as I mentioned, faithless Pasha flirted with her shamelessly. "Lifeboat material" is Jules' highest compliment . . . it means someone possesses a skill that would be useful to Jules in a life or death situation. Most of us dream of desert islands and what we'll take there. But Jules sees only disaster, hence the lifeboat. With my former husband it is black or white, life or death. Never paradise with a favorite book or piece of music. Just life and death.

Pasha arched his back. There's a pose in yoga called the cat stretch and that's exactly what he's doing. Lydia has a naturally flexible spine; I noticed that right away at yoga class, though a rank beginner she was excellent at the cat stretch. Funny, because Lydia and Pasha are quite a bit alike. Just like Lydia and I are alike in certain ways. Both are graceful, decorative, radiate an air of content, and are sneaky. Just for the record, I'm graceful and I'm decorative, certainly when I was her age, but never content. Not when I lived there, never for long. And admittedly, I'm sneaky too. Which is why, of course, I was on the outside looking in and not inside where they are.

Odd, how sound travels. I thought I heard cutlery against plates. Which meant that Jules and Lydia were having dinner . . . to my taste, a little late. But I never said Lydia was exactly like me, just enough like me to make us all feel completely comfortable. Jules most of all. Pasha was no longer at the front window. No doubt, he was heading for the warmer dining room and the smell of food. I was hungry suddenly, wondering what they were having. I rarely eat dinner these days, just a bite of this or that, a banana and a couple of crackers, some store-bought soup. I always fantasized about getting to eat exactly what I want when I want to, but missing a meal is never as satisfying as the fantasy that you get to. You find that out rather quickly.

I wonder if Lydia shares food with Pasha. When she makes herself a tuna sandwich, does she section off a chunk without mayonnaise for his little blue and white dish? And shrimp? Jules and Pasha both adore shrimp. Or does Lydia just throw him the scraps as most people do? Dear Pasha! When the twins grew up, I used to sing the same little songs to him I once sang to my boys when they were toddlers in their tub. I do hope Lydia shares food with him. She probably did in the beginning to copy me. If you do something for a little while, often it becomes a habit. Indeed, I was aware from the beginning how Lydia studied the way I did things. At first, I thought, out of deep sympathy and liking for me, the older, more sophisticated woman. And then after she fell in love with Jules, she studied me—she naturally would do better! Maybe in a certain sense I was her role model for a time, her mentor. Me, a role model? Then again, from what she told me, I was much better than her own mother. I found her a husband, didn't I?

At first it was enough for me to stand on the sidewalk in front of the living room windows. But soon curiosity got the upper hand. Growing bolder, I quietly approached the dining room windows at the side of the house. Now, I was no longer a casual nobody walking down the street, but something of a Peeping Tom. In my case, a Peeping Harriet. It's not the house after all, or

Pasha, it's them I wanted to see!

Just as this came to me, I was enveloped in a velvety silence. Like a good sauce, silence has a certain texture. Not a single car engine could be heard, so rare in LA, particularly in the densely populated communities near the beach. Now another chill passed down my spine ... goose bumps on my arms. I heard a laugh I have no trouble recognizing as Lydia's. Voice recognition must be like taste recognition. You hear the sound; you put the taste on your tongue. That's lemon, that's Lydia. There were months when I knew her well, and yes, I studied her, just as she studied me. I would know her laugh anywhere. All this time with Jules and she can still laugh? Lydia *is* lifeboat material. I moved quickly along the side of the house toward that low, delightful laugh. Standing a little away, I stared in the window. I don't consciously want her to see me, but I couldn't seem to budge; in fact, I stood like an old tree with roots digging deep into the ground. At that moment, it would have taken a bolt of lightning to budge me.

There she was! Young, gorgeous, raven-haired Lydia. She was sitting at my old kitchen table with her smartphone up to her ear, the characteristic pose of the twenty-first century. Will art reflecting our time capture this? I'm old enough to remember not only the good old days when the landline reigned supreme, but a time when people walking down the street having one-way conversations were headed for a rendezvous with the nut house, not a dinner date.

Even from out there, I could see the place was a mess. My old dining table was a junk heap. When I lived there, a platter with seasonal fruit adorned the center. I never let newspapers or books pile up. Most of the time, there were flowers. And not just any old flowers, ones carefully bought at the farmers' market from the organic vendor who didn't use sprays. I liked the look of a single flower stem pushed into an amber vanilla bottle; these I scattered about. I had so many of them left over from all my baking. If I didn't have flowers, I stuck my homegrown herbs in. What a hausfrau I was. A real *balabusta*, Jules would laughingly call me. Every lifeboat needs a balabusta.

There was a movie playing on the flat screen mounted on the wall. Lydia's wide, luminous eyes were following its every move—like my boys, she's a genius at multi-tasking. Talk, watch, eat, stare at the computer screen, and up at the television screen, probably she's got a remote in hand too. Lydia's a screenwriter, so she was no doubt watching carefully as she ate takeout from different containers. The cutlery sound on plates must have been coming from another house, or I was having an auditory hallucination, or perhaps a little reunion with the old sounds that used to emanate from in there. Memories linger, why not sounds and smells too?

And where was Jules? Still working late? Even with this young hot thing waiting for him at home? And when he did come home, was it takeout (Lydia would say takeaway) now that the balabusta had been thrown off the lifeboat?

My eyes traveled to the corner of the kitchen near the red wall phone and the gleaming Sub-Zero. I knew it was there, but I couldn't really make out the big color glossy of him. He took it himself, standing by the Harley with helmet in hand, a roguish smile on his handsome face. So Jules! Yes, he must have ridden the Harley to work. That's why the Beemer was parked in the driveway; he'd taken the darker, far more dangerous sibling to work. Jules' Harley, purchased in my last year there, was the penultimate irreconcilable difference. As much as he loved the Harley, that's how much I hated the shiny gleaming thing and refused to ever ride on it. Lydia, being young and bold and all too eager to put her arms around my husband and to press her high, firm breasts onto him, went riding right away. She even got herself a leather jacket. Or perhaps it was Jules who got her the leather jacket, now that I think of it. He offered to buy me one, "go to Beverly Hills, woman, and charge it to me!" Jules almost never said, "charge it to me!" But I didn't take him up on his offer.

"I'm not the black leather jacket type," I told him.

Did I hear the roar of a distant motorcycle coming my way? Or was it just the engine of my memory? I didn't want to be caught there, what would I say? I'm a ghost?

If he caught me, he probably wouldn't be surprised. I can hear him say, "You can go home, now, Harriet, end of conversation!"

In fact, that's exactly what I decided to do, go home, such as it was. But as I walked the familiar suburban streets that suddenly didn't feel so familiar anymore, I couldn't find my car. I guess I was in more or less a state of shock seeing the old place, and seeing her in my place. And like it or not, I found myself back with Jules in our New York apartment in the old, old days.

"Harriet, I've told you a million times, there's nothing I can do about it! End of conversation!"

"Who are you, the speech police? Now you can talk. Now you can't talk?"

"Lower your voice, the neighbors can hear you. You'll wake up the babies."

"I will not wake up the babies, they sleep like rocks!"

"A man can't get any peace and quiet in his own home. I had a horrible day. I'm sick of New York. I'm sick of shooting commercials. I'm sick of the subway.

If I get this movie, we're moving to California."

"If we move to California, I'll lose all my customers."

"You'll make new ones."

"What if I don't? What if I'm just stuck with the babies in the I Love Lucy hotel waiting for you to come home—I don't even have a driver's license anymore."

"Harriet, for the love of God, give it a rest. What happened to you? You used to be so skinny and sweet?"

"Are you calling me fat?"

"Who said anything about fat?"

"You said I used to be so skinny and sweet!"

"You were."

"And what am I now, fat and mean?"

"Lower your voice!"

"My voice is low; I'm just expressing my consternation."

"You're so negative!"

"No, I'm not, I'm worried!"

"Shooting movies would be so much better than shooting commercials. Don't you want me to be happy?"

"Of course I want you to be happy."

"Good, that means we have to stick together."

And stick together we did. For years and years. Even if Jules didn't exactly fulfill his adhesive part of the bargain and was away on location when the boys took their first steps; when their bottom teeth grew in on the same night. When Dan got beaten up at school when he was five, it was my friend Lisa and I who taught him how to punch back.

"Where's Daddy?" the boys cried. "How come he's never home?"

Just when we were giving up hope, Jules would magically appear. There he would be with a big smile on his face, carrying tricycles for the boys, then bicycles. He taught each one to drive the stick shift, just like he taught me when we finally gave up our apartment in New York and moved to California the year the boys turned six.

Two

I CAN'T SEEM TO COME BACK TO THE PRESENT. IT's probably all the endless things I must do in the next days before I board the plane for New York. My mind wants to escape. It seems vitally important to know exactly when this whole thing started. First it was Lydia and me. Then it became Lydia and me and Jules. Two's company and three's a crowd, especially when there are urges. It didn't take long for Mother Nature to bring Lydia and Jules together and push me away. Have I mentioned I was the one who found Lydia? I was the one who brought the biological time bomb into the house. Lydia made no secret of the fact that she was longing for a house and a husband and a baby. When I brought her home that first day, she even looked around and said, "You've got it all! Everything I'd sell my soul for. I bet your husband is even handsome!"

Ticktock, ticktock, the time bomb was ticking away as relentlessly as the big kitchen clock that hung on the wall.

With the brilliant clarity of hindsight, I can see the fulcrum point of change occurred not after my boys went to college but right before. I was slicing onions when I started to cry on the set of my show, *Healthy Harriet*, which tapes at six in the morning, two days a week.

"My boys are leaving home. Empty-nest soup is what I'll be making for Jules and me. Where did the time go? How many meals have I made in eighteen years? I tried to calculate the other day."

I remember putting down my chopping blade. Mine was a middling- to low-rated show. I was a worker, not a star, and certainly not one with an attitude. I make healthy food, which in case anyone is interested, is not sexy and no one cares about it. I cracked a few jokes; I smiled for the camera. I was lucky I had a show at all and didn't have to do catering. It was totally unlike me to start to cry in the middle of chopping. And I mean sobbing, with tears running down my cheeks. A startled technician ran to the set with a tissue. Then I composed myself. Which, being me, was much easier to do than showing my real feelings. I even managed to smile.

"Forget the empty nest; let's try this another way . . ."

So we did another take and I made no mention of the empty nest.

"The secret to a good vegetarian soup is caramelized onion...." I went about browning some onions in the trusty frying pan I used on the set.

"I use olive oil with just a speck of butter—a speck is quite healthy actually, lots of vitamin E."

The camera came in close on me and the onions sizzling nicely in the pan.

"How long does it take to caramelize onions? Well I think of it as a road trip with young children: When are we going to get there? Are they brown yet?"

This produced a few twitters of laughter from the crew; they were generally very kind to me when I tried to work in a little humor.

Later at home, I was still convulsed with sadness. I felt like someone had socked me in the solar plexus. Not that I had time to be sad. There was so much to do before all of us boarded the plane the next day. We were going to drop Sam first in New York, and stay overnight at Jules' mother's apartment in the city. Then Jules and I were flying with Dan to Chicago the day after that. It was the first time in years and years our family was actually going to do something together away from home.

I ran up the stairs, stood in front of Sam's

door, and knocked.

"Sam?"

Inside, I knew, my beautiful Sam would be lying in his bed, zonked out at eleven something in the morning with his earphones on. Nothing much packed or organized, every single solitary thing left to the last moment.

I shrieked, "Sammy, open up or you're busted!"

"Okay, you can come in."

I entered and looked around. The suitcases weren't even opened. I wasn't going to get in a fight with Sam on his last official day at home. Besides, I rarely fought with Sam. He was too charming and manipulative to fight with me.

"Your hair looks nice, Ma."

I smiled, though I knew I was getting played.

"You're only being sweet because you're high. It's eleven in the morning and you're in bed high. This does not bode well for your future!"

Sam sat up and pulled at the top sheet to cover himself. He already had a few hairs on his chest. Sam with hair on his chest did not seem possible. But I had felt this way when those first dark, wispy hairs began to sprout on both twins' upper lips, and now I was used to their shaving. God protect us, the old saying goes, from what we can grow used to.

"It's your fault. I'm rebelling against all your

healthy food and clean living!"

"You're nowhere near packed. Do you want me to help you? If you don't want me, Valentina would be happy to. Just get up and get dressed for heaven's sake!"

Sam plugged his earphones back in. "Cool it, Ma. It's all good. It's all okay."

"But you've got so much to do."

"End of conversation, Harriet!"

Sam said this laughingly, because "end of conversation" was a joke around our house. We were always imitating Jules behind his back, my boys and I.

I turned, left his room, and went to stand in front of Dan's door.

Dan was born first, and on the surface he's a lot less of a mess than his twin brother. His room was spectacularly tidy for a teenager, or anybody of any age for that matter. I knew when Dan let me in I'd see everything was organized and ready to go. Dan couldn't wait to get out of the house. And though it pains me to admit this, I was even a little glad at the prospect myself.

I could smell the cigarette smoke from where I stood. I imagined Dan walking to the window where the screen was open and putting out his lit cigarette. Whenever I walked by the side of the house under his window, it smelled like a humidor.

"Okay, you can come in now."

I walked in and smiled, trying to be casual and friendly. I was always trying to be casual and friendly with Dan, and we both knew I was faking it. What I really wanted to do was throw a fit and scream, "What the fuck happened to us, Dan? What the fuck happened to you? You're a stuffed shirt with no sense of humor and I wasn't such a horrible mother for you to hate me so much."

I looked around at his room, which already seemed to be empty. Everything was packed, tidied, and in order. It reminded me of a smoking room at a hotel.

"I know you don't need help packing. But is there anything else I can do?"

"No. End of conversation!"

There was no laugh in his voice. Dan was seriously channeling Jules. Perhaps even beating out his father's cold, confident way of cutting off any possible flow of information or feeling—never mind love.

And also channeling that what-the-fuck look I knew so well.

"I'm your mom; I'm just trying to get close before you go."

Dan looked me squarely in the face, something he wasn't in the habit of doing.

"You might as well know this now. If I don't like it at school, I'm enlisting. Understand?

With my grades, I can go in as an officer."

This was the first I'd heard of this wretched idea. Though the minute he told me, I could actually see it in my mind's eye: my stern, unhappy boy—the more sensitive of the twins, who used to write the most beautiful poetry when he was a little boy—morph into some four-star general with medals on his chest. Yes, I could even hear him calling out, "Atten-tun!"

I suppose my face must have shown my devastation. Dan surprised me by acting like a human being for the first time in months.

"I didn't say I was doing it. I'm just saying it's a possibility."

For the second time that day I started to cry. Me, who had not shed a tear in years. "Killing people is the end of possibility. And the food sucks."

"Just fucking leave me alone and leave my room!"

I turned and left. What I wanted to do was flip him off. What I ended up doing was saluting him. Then I closed the door and stood cringing in the doorway.

Downstairs, Valentina, my darling housekeeper, was sedulously mincing ginger with the small Global, her favorite knife. She was doing such a good job; the ginger was almost in paste form.

Valentina is young, not quite thirty, and beautiful, with thick dark hair and gorgeous eyes. She came to me when she was eighteen, just after Angel was born.

When Jules' mother came for her yearly visit to the coast to see Jules and his half brother Freeman, she would invariably chide me with, "What were thinking when you hired her, Harriet?"

"Jules isn't interested in Valentina, Gloria."

"How do you know?"

"Because I know."

"But how can you be sure?"

Jules always hid his toothbrush before Valentina arrived. He didn't like her changing "our bed" and made me swear I would do it myself. He didn't want her folding his socks, his underwear, and he didn't want her going in his closet. Though she never said so, I thought the feeling was mutual: natural born enemies.

"That's some of the best looking minced ginger I've ever seen," I told her truthfully. "You could be a professional sous-chef."

I sat down at the kitchen table.

"Sam's stoned and Dan's threatening to enlist in the military."

"They trying to be men, Harriet."

I felt like crying again. In fact, I put my head down on the table.

"I lost them both somewhere between kindergarten and condoms. Sam worries me a lot less than Dan even though he seems to be high all the time, at least he appears to be having fun."

"I know what you mean."

Paranoid suddenly, I picked my head up. "Do you know something I don't know?"

Valentina shook her head. "What you need me to do?"

"Sit down," I told her, "talk to me. Have a cup of tea. We haven't visited in a while. How's Angel? How's Jesus?"

Valentina settled herself in.

"Jesus has work this week."

Valentina hastily crossed herself and began to finger the crucifix around her neck. My high school years were spent at a convent so I did the same, minus the cross fondling, thinking that apart from the pedophile priests and the no birth control, how enormously comforting it must be to be Catholic. The rosaries, the beautiful cathedrals, the release of confession.

"Angel didn't do so good in summer school. They putting him back."

I felt a huge rush of guilt wrap its way around my ribcage, where the empty-nest pain now seemed to have taken up permanent residence.

My sons had money behind them, health care, and were headed to nationally ranked colleges. What was going to happen to Angel in free clinics and the shitty schools I never had to subject the twins to?

Just then the wall phone rang.

It was Jules. He sounded desperately rushed—'Only five seconds' before he had to go back on the set. The gist of it was, though he felt really terrible, and was thinking he better go back to therapy because he didn't know how he got in these situations, disappointing people, he couldn't take the boys to school tomorrow. Something about the airdate, something about the network, something about the director who was thirteen years old and was a total fucking moron—on a good day! I'd heard this tale in many different variations over the years and I was always surprised anew, as though it was the first time it had happened.

Apparently Jules had just phoned the boys himself. Dan first, because everybody always puts Dan first. If you don't, he accuses you of never putting him first.

"Did you tell Gloria?"

"No," Jules panted, "I don't have time. The director's coming in five minutes. You'll have to tell her for me."

"So I have to stay with your mother myself?"

"Harriet, I'll make it up to you, I swear it!"

I banged down the phone. Furious. How many times did I bang the phone down furious? I never learned to step away. To take a deep breath or to ask myself what's really going on here? I was furious. And I stayed furious. And furious people don't do anything but rage, get over it, and then rage again.

Valentina was looking at me pityingly.

"They moved the airdate on the show Jules is shooting. He's not coming with us."

"They never do what they say."

"Jesus does what you say. He respects you."

"I train him to be scared, Harriet. You can't train Jules. He too stubborn. He won't listen. He only thinking about Jules."

Still livid, I closed my eyes, "I just don't get it. . . ."

"Harriet," Valentina whispered.

"Yes, Valentina?"

"He only thinking about Jules."

Later that day, I knocked at Dan's door again.

"Come in," he called out, as if it was a stranger outside, not me.

"So I guess you heard the news?"

"What news?"

"About your Dad?"

"It wasn't news to me. You always act surprised. I never thought Dad was going to come to begin with. He always craps out at the last moment."

"You and I will take Sam to school. We'll stay at Gloria's. Then I'll take you to school.

We'll have a great time! There's eight zillion restaurants we can go to."

"I'm going by myself. I planned to go by myself all along. I knew he wouldn't come."

Just then Dan's phone went off. Dan's signal was a dirge, depressing and atonal, as if he was never going to hear good news. Where on earth had he located such a horrible ringtone?

"Hey, Dad."

My son listened, then nodded. I saw him smile for the first time in a long time.

"That's great! Hey thanks, Pop."

Dan tapped his phone. Then Sam burst in.

"Did Dad call you?"

"Affirmative."

I looked from one happy son to the other.

"What's going on?"

"You two are staying put. The old man is going to give us the money he would have spent on meals and plane fare."

I had wondered about the plane fare. Jules must have paid the extra bucks for flight insurance knowing he would probably crap out. I was fuming, thinking that he had better not have cancelled my seat.

"I'm still coming!" I told my boys.

Sam came over and put his arm around me. The left one with the giant tattoo of a German Shepherd head on his outer, very pumped up bicep.

"Why a German Shepherd?" I had asked him when he showed the horrible thing to me—and went on to tell me he had put it on his/our charge card.

"I always wanted a dog."

Another thing to feel guilty about.

"Mom, if Dad isn't coming, neither are you. We need the extra money. You know how cheap Jules is."

I looked from one beaming countenance to the other. I guess I knew then they didn't really care if I came to college to set up their rooms. Sure, they would put up with me, but it's freedom they wanted, freedom of course with their bills paid. I could relate to that, isn't that what we all want, after all?

"Last chance!" I was teasing, of course, but some of me was serious. "So I guess you'd rather have the money, huh?"

Sam nodded sheepishly. Dan to his credit managed to look sheepish as well. I could tell they were excited beneath their kind show of good manners. Because it was written all over both my boys' faces: *Fucking A, baby! Free at last!*

"Okay, okay!" I said finally. "So be it!"

The next day, Dan and I drove Sam to the airport. We parked the car in the lot, and as I was preparing to take him in, Sam hugged me and told me he loved me, but not to come in. Dan helped him with his luggage and I stayed in the car lot with the empty-nest pain throbbing in my gut.

The day after that, Dan ordered a taxi to pick him up at home because he refused to go through the guilt trip (his choice of words) I was sure to lay on him at the airport. He didn't hug me or tell me that he loved me. He just looked miserable. But I could see it had something to do with the trouble he was having making this big separation. I helped him schlep the suitcases to the taxi. Only then, before he slipped in the door, did he turn, meet my eyes for a moment, and give me a little wave of the hand. It wasn't a cheerful windshield wiper wave of the boy who wanted his freedom—but a sad little flutter of his long, thin fingers, like a bird struggling off the ground, unable to fly.

After he left, I spent hours walking from room to room in my house, looking around. I took down all the schedules and crap that was cluttering the Sub-Zero and gave it a good polish. How grown up it looked, how sophisticated. I even took down all the tiny little magnets I liked so much and that Jules hated and was always having a fit about.

"What if one falls in our food? What if Pasha eats one? I want you to buy magnets the size of silver dollars. Someone could die from one of these!"

Life and death. Black and white. At five, instead of starting dinner for me and the boys, I slung my mat bag over my shoulder and headed to yoga. I could even walk because I had the time. On the walk home, I picked up some take-out sushi, since I assumed Jules would be eating on the set with the 'thirteen-year-old moron director' and the rest of the motley crew who never went home to dinner either.

I felt wonderfully wicked eating the sushi in front of the TV set all by myself, with just Pasha to share with. I was pleased I had the foresight to ask for plenty of extra ginger, which I didn't have to share with the cat. Eating in front of the TV is strictly taboo at my house. As is order-in pizza, order-in anything for that matter, as well as junk food, soda, the list goes on and on. No wonder the boys were happy to be away from me! I was such a rigid stick-in-the-mud.

In their earlier years, before all the big, ugly reports came out about MacDonald's and Burger King and the quality of the meat they were purveying, I used to take them once a month to the fast food restaurant of their choice and even join them. Now, of course, since they are skinny and healthy and don't have any fillings, I feel justified in my actions and glad that I stopped giving in even once a month.

The trumpets for *Masterpiece Theatre* were

doing their thing when I heard the scrape of Jules' chock outside the window sometime later.

Pasha thumped down and went to greet Jules as he always did.

"Hi," I called out, "you're home early."

"We wrapped early."

"Oh," I said.

"You eat?"

"Yes."

"Anything left for me?"

"I had takeout."

"Takeout? Standards are slipping around here."

I didn't say anything. I continued to stare at the screen. For the record, I didn't have the remotest idea what I was watching. I was so overwhelmed with all sorts of new sensations—sensations that seemed to be streaming through me as though I was in a sci-fi movie with colorful lights and laser beams.

"Harriet? What's going on?"

Again I didn't answer. Or jump to attention (my default position) to show Jules that the balabusta was in the lifeboat, ready to do her thing. And, in fact, in one part of my mind, I could already see the little ad hoc feast I would assemble in less than half an hour, as I had hundreds of times before. Tomatoes were still in season and we had them. There were onions, garlic, and mushrooms, and wedges of two kinds of grating cheese. Not to mention jars of my own preserved peppers ready to dump over rice or pasta. And fresh herbs to garnish with. Of course there was plenty of frozen stuff ready to nuke. But Jules didn't like nuked food.

Still, I didn't budge.

I was exquisitely aware of the tremendous amount of effort it took not to jump up and head for the kitchen, peppy as Pavlov's dog. I sat perfectly still, taking the smallest little breaths in and out of my nose, only just enough to get air in. By now the special effects had worn off. And I was starting to feel like a political prisoner hiding in a closet, terrified that any second the authorities would discover I was here and haul me away.

I mention terror because it was a form of fear. And not of Jules, really—I guess I thought I knew Jules inside and out, like that prisoner knows the inside of the closet—I was afraid of myself and what was happening to me. This new-found stubbornness was alien; I had no idea these feelings resided in me. Feelings that didn't make me comfortable at all.

Nevertheless, I continued to sit there watching the screen. The room was quiet, just the British-y voices of the show hosts on the screen. It was unheard of for me to be watching TV at such an hour. Or any hour, come to that. I was always trying to go to sleep early so I could wake up at 4:00 for my show.

Jules sat down. He put his arm around me and started kissing my neck. Soon I was underneath him on the living room couch.

"We haven't fucked on the couch in eighteen years." He said this aloud, in the kind of voice you use when you know no one can overhear. "In fact, I think we should have another kid. It's lonely around here; I feel old!"

Three

"Why are we here?"

"You go first, Harriet, since it's your idea."

"I thought we could talk some things out. We don't communicate very well. I get so frustrated I start screaming in the shower. I can't help myself, I just open my mouth and out it comes, this bloodcurdling sound."

Both of us were in Jim's very nice commodious office having a session of marriage counseling. I had remembered Jim's name. An old customer of mine back in the catering days had claimed Jim was a genius and had "saved" their marriage.

A genius is just what we needed.

"And Jules, what do you do when Harriet starts her bloodcurdling screaming?"

I looked at Jules, who, for perhaps the first time since we met twenty years ago, had nothing to say. No opinions. No rants. This Jim *was* a genius. He could silence Jules, whose ears seemed to be lying back. I was so pleased, I started to giggle.

"Are you scared when she screams?"

Jules nodded his head.

"Do you think it means Harriet needs some attention?"

Jim looked from Jules to me. Then back to Jules. I was still giggling.

"Laughter is generally a good sign in a relationship. But Harriet, are you laughing because you think this is funny or because you're nervous?"

"Nervous," I confessed. And began to giggle anew.

"Jules, Harriet's laughing, but you look a little uncomfortable. Would you like to talk about it?"

"You're right!" Jules told our marriage counselor. "I'm very uncomfortable. I don't like my chair. How come you get the good chair, and I get the broken one?"

Jules squirmed around some more. Then he got up and went for another chair in the room and dragged it over. This he sat on, wiggled his ass a bit, and looked at our marriage counselor with real disgust.

Jim asked kindly, "Do you think I deliberately gave you a broken chair?"

"I don't see you sitting on it."

Calm, seen-it-all Genius Jim, apparently hadn't seen Jules. His pale skin was turning a little pink. His voice was getting higher pitched with every word. No doubt his IQ was dropping lower and lower by the second.

"Jules, I sit in *my* chair."

"And you give me the shit one and expect me to just sit here pretending it's comfortable, possibly hurting my back. Hostile if you ask me."

"What do you want me to do, Jules?"

I watched Jules get to his feet.

"Switch with me! I'll take your chair and you sit in the uncomfortable one."

"You can't sit in my chair, it's my chair."

Jim asked us a few more questions, but it was clear that he was not the man for the job; Jules could out-talk, out-maneuver, and push Genius Jim's buttons without much effort. At the end of our session, I wrote Jim a check for two hundred and fifty dollars, about a quarter of the cost of the new desk chair I'd been yearning to buy myself ever since I saw it in a magazine. It was black mesh, very comfortable, Italian, and would, I know, give me far more pleasure and consolation than marriage counseling with Jules and Jim.

We walked out together. Jules was very cheerful. And once again his usual voluble self.

"Did you see the way he fell apart just because I wanted his chair? Where did you get his name, I don't think he's so smart. Shrinks are supposed to be Jewish. No one in their right mind would go to a blond shrink who wears boating shoes."

"Those were loafers not boating shoes, Jules."

"What's the fucking difference? He was a blond, beardless moron. Find someone else."

"You did the same thing the last time. You said she and I would gang up against you. That's why I got a man this time. You just won't cooperate."

"You're the one to talk about cooperation. I want another kid. I'm willing to go through all the time and expense if I can't get you knocked up normally. And you say no, you want a dog."

"You're always gone. You wouldn't help me. I raised the twins by myself."

"Have a little faith. I might surprise you."

"Surprise me and do what?"

"I don't know. Try a little harder, be a better father."

"Like how would you try? Can you be a little more specific?"

We were at the car by then. I was driving home with Jules because I'd walked there.

"Would you wake up in the middle of the night and change diapers?"

Jules didn't say anything.

"Would you go for PTA meetings?"

Jules didn't say anything.

"How about taking them off to college? If we go through fertility stuff we are far more likely to have more twins! Would you take this set off to college?"

"The schedule was unclear, Harriet. It was totally out of my control."

"It's always out of your control when you don't want to do something."

"Some women would be flattered their husbands still want them."

"I am flattered. I just don't want another child. There's something else too. I got a call today about a really interesting job. A consultant on a panel that's funded by a food company that wants to promote healthy food and all the stuff I do. Or at least pretend to, but it comes to the same thing in the end."

"What about *Healthy Harriet?*"

"I could quit after the holidays when the replacements come in. Who knows, they might not even renew my show. I hate being in front of the camera, you know that. Besides, no one watches my show, it's a joke. You know I'm always worried about it getting cancelled."

"So take the job. They can't fire women anymore when they get pregnant. It's not PC. What are they offering?"

When I told him, he looked respectful.

"You could buy me a sailboat. I'll show you the one I want. Let's go to the marina this weekend."

"Only trouble is, the job's in New York."

We were still standing in the parking lot on the roof of Jim's building. That grayish-brown light that permeates LA in late August obscured any chance of blue in the sky. It was hot and dry, "rattlesnake weather" is what I called it.

"If you remember, we tried the bicoastal thing, when the boys were babies. It didn't work."

"It didn't work with children, Jules. It could work with adults, provided one of them agrees to grow up. And we'd get to see the boys more."

"I can't believe you spring this on me when I've got so much on my mind. You demand I come to this moron therapist with the broken chairs. And now this. I told you we're doing reshoots. You're so selfish; you're always putting yourself first. But by all means, get a dog. Are you going to take the fucking dog with you to New York? And don't expect me to pick up its fucking warm dog shit!"

We got in the car and drove in silence for a bit. A Prius cut Jules off. And he flew into a rage, honking his horn and shouting out the window.

"Hey you! Fuck you! Goddamn LA driver, that cock bite's lucky I'm not armed. Have you ever noticed the most hostile drivers in the world drive the PC Prius? I hate them. They're worse than Brentwood housewives in SUVs."

"So let's move back to New York. You can get work there and I'll fly back here when you get gigs. Public transportation, Jules. None of this!"

Jules put the transmission in third gear.

"What, are you nuts, woman? I grew up riding the subway. I've had enough of that!

Animals behind bars. Cats crying. Dogs yipping pitifully. Cellblock after cellblock of Chihuahuas. According to my guide, Chihuahuas are very hard to handle. That movie about the Beverly Hills Chihuahuas spurred so many people to buy them then abandon them. How does one do that? Willingly consign a creature to the pound? No sunshine, no grass, no cushions, certainly no special food like Pasha was used to. No, I had never before been to the pound. And when I left empty-handed, having filled out all the forms, I didn't want to go to one again. It was too depressing.

I did the thing you aren't supposed to ever do. The evil act that promotes puppy mills: I found my dog at a pet store. I went in to buy Pasha some of his special organic cat cereal that I mix with fresh meat, and I came out with Marco, whom I named on the spot; a baby Jack Russell Terrier with a caramel-colored silky head, a whipped cream-colored body, and one little matching caramel spot on the left side of his body. He was an older pup, the runt of his litter, and according to the man who owned the pet store, already housebroken.

Indeed he *was* housebroken. In fact he was the funniest, cutest, most heart-wrenchingly wonderful dog that even Jules did the unthinkable: he fell in love with Marco too. And proclaimed that every lifeboat needs a dog to cheer everybody up.

Yes, Jules adored little Marco. And when Marco rose from his small bed at the foot of our bed, he went to Jules' side and jumped up and down. And though Jules, of course, waited for me to get up and take Marco out, he was my partner in the doggy days far more than he was ever one in the twin baby days. And he took it upon himself to take the last walk of the day with Marco and let me go to bed early. He even made a few street friends. I noticed at once that little Marco was a total chick magnet. In fact peppy Marco and peppy Jules looked a little alike, strutting around with their chests puffed up.

The only living creature who felt differently was the cat. Though Marco tried his best to win Pasha over, wagging his tail, jumping up and down in the air, even once moving aside so

Pasha could drink out of his water dish, the cat remained steadfastly unfazed by the new addition to our household.

Of course, I couldn't resist making dog biscuits. I even dedicated a whole show to making healthy dog food and healthy dog treats. Lots of people liked it—I received the kind of attention my producers had been hoping for all along. It's something I've noticed for years. People who have no interest in staying in shape and feeding themselves good food are vitally concerned about doing the right thing—or perhaps the thing they should be doing for themselves—for their pets. Healthy living by proxy with the animals.

Still I couldn't have been happier with this brief new turn of affairs. Though I didn't mention it to Jules, I felt like saying, "Isn't this better than having another baby?"

But I restrained myself. Apart from claiming he had a condom on when he didn't, he let the baby thing drop once Marco came into our life. I even caught him telling Marco, "You're Daddy's little boy."

I told the New York people I couldn't take the job right away, and they said to keep them in mind. Whenever you don't want something, I always notice they want you and want you badly. They claimed they were interested in healthy pet food too.

Four

IT'S NOT SURPRISING THAT I MET LYDIA AT YOGA. WHERE else did I go regularly other than work, the grocery store, and the farmers' market? She put her mat down next to mine and we smiled at each other, the way yoga people do.

I took up practicing in the summer before the boys entered their senior year of high school. I heard it helped you sleep, and if I hung around the house at the dinner hour cooking and serving, the boys and I would invariably start shrieking at one another. That year, Jules was working thirty miles away on some show shot on a horse ranch mostly at night. Wednesday night he was home, and he generally spent it in bed with a tray and the remote control. Once in a while, he and the boys went out to this revolting Mexican restaurant they all love and I won't go near. Otherwise, he was gone except on the weekends when he slept, being understandably exhausted from the night shoots. Three mornings a week before dawn, Jules and I would cross paths in the kitchen: me with my commuter's mug of café au lait on my way to the cable studio for *Healthy Harriet*, Jules on his way to the kitchen for his Irish oatmeal before hitting the sack. (The oatmeal everybody loved was made the night before in the Crock-pot.) Looking back, it is remarkable how often Jules landed gigs that either sent him on location or put him in an entire other stratosphere schedulewise from the rest of us.

Once I started yoga, I was hooked almost right away and began going into down dogs in the kitchen and soon handstands against the door that led to the laundry room. When I took the boys for their college tours, I remember googling yoga studios in the towns we visited. Like cooking, it kept me sane. And gave me something to look forward to. And it wasn't solitary like running. I liked the chanting. The bowing and the Namaste—I particularly loved the one chant we repeated three times: *Loca Samasta Sukihino Bhvantu.* May all beings everywhere be happy and free from suffering.

By that point I must have begun to realize, subconsciously at least, that as much as I loved him, I was much happier and the boys acted better when Jules wasn't around. What a revelation! For years I had been in the habit of thinking the problem was that Jules was gone most of the time and we all missed him. Granted we did miss him, especially in those first few years in LA when they were young and I didn't know a soul and I had to start all over again work-wise. Though I do remember sort of putting it together, that the horrible pains that tightened my neck muscles and sent me to the chiropractor for adjustments only happened when Jules was at home. When he was around, I not only felt sort of queasy, I could literally feel the chords of my neck tightening like the reins of a workhorse.

The Jules Effect wasn't a whole lot more salubrious on the boys. In fact Sam started having the same neck problems I did. Maybe it was his violin, maybe not. I'm not trying to say things were perfect between the boys and me. Especially Dan and me. Certainly we fought when I hung around serving them dinner and when I fussed like they were ten years old. However, when I stopped doing that, we were much better. I say all this because the combination of just leaving them food and not fussing over them, realizing I didn't miss Jules, realizing they didn't miss Jules, doing yoga, and finally (when they left home and the coast was clear) meeting Lydia—were like finding the essential fixings for a good stock, and the basis for what I cooked up. The spontaneous orgasm at yoga probably didn't hurt either. A little giftie from the universe, a sort of *hey, look, it can happen again, maybe not in the way you think, but it can happen.*

Dinnertime yoga in LA—and probably everywhere else too—is primarily practiced by single and/or divorced women. If I were a guy on the make, that's the first place I'd go: women who do a lot of yoga have great bodies and I even stopped shouting (except in the shower) when I got hooked. But the men at yoga are usually few and far between and often gay. That or AA. It didn't take me long to discover not only was I one of the least limber in class, I was also the only woman there who actually lived with her husband and kids. Certainly my role at home was quite different than it had been before—the real change had come when they got their driver's licenses. However, I still considered myself a mom. And I did what moms do everywhere, whether their day jobs are over or not. I planned the meals, did the shopping, cooked what they liked, ran the house, showed up at school functions and bought them things, tried to get them to talk to me—and now that they were older, watched for signs of drugs, though I generally avoided signs of sex. A far cry from the old days when there was all this plus driving, plus organized sports, music lessons, and the rest of it. Since I'm trying to tell it like it was, did I mind that I wasn't so fucking central anymore? Not really. Sometimes I felt wistful for the early years, particularly when I looked at the lines around my face. But like a lot of women, I was dead-tired from too many years of doing too much cooking/managing/scheduling. Yoga gave me a place to go and something to get good at, though I'll never be really good at it in the way I would have been had I started in my twenties.

Randy, who was teaching the night I met Lydia, was a mixed-race hunk, twenty-four years old with blond dreadlocks, golden skin, and shoulders that stretched from east to west.

"*Supta Badda Konasana* . . . lie flat on your back. Put the soles of your feet together and let your knees relax and sink toward the floor. Good. Bring your awareness to your groin. And Breathe. Breathe!"

I suspect Randy must have had that effect on others because unless you got there early and put your mat down, you couldn't get a place. And, after it happened to me, I figured it was probably happening at yoga centers all over the country, and was at least in part responsible for the huge surge in popularity.

It makes perfect sense, when you're lying there, soles of the feet together, thighs spread, breathing into the sex organs that once in a while someone will get off.

OMMMMMMM!

When the class rang out with the chorus of OM, I'm almost sure I came forth with an AHHHM. Just for the record, the big O during the big OM has never happened since then, though I have gotten close a few times. And I still do yoga almost every day. And I'll never know whether Lydia knew what was happening on the mat next to her.

"How often do you come?" she asked in her melodious English voice. Not of course what she meant, still strangely apposite for the first thing she said to me.

"Every day if I can. I'm hooked, how about you?"

"I'm a rank beginner. I'm Lydia, by the way."

"I'm Harriet."

We didn't shake hands. We were schlepping our mats and navigating down the stairs and onto the street. When we hit the lit sidewalk, she did a little start.

"Healthy Harriet!"

I smiled.

"You taught me to make brown rice with mung beans, carrots, ginger, and ghee."

"I'm so pleased!" I told her and it was true. It wasn't that she recognized my dubious status as the most minor of food network hosts. It was the certainty right away that this beautiful, obviously highly intelligent creature with the gorgeous English accent seemed to approve of me and get me. I felt the same way about her too. We were natural-born friends.

"Good old mung!" I replied. "I've got that cooking at home in the rice cooker."

Somewhat later, with Pasha in her lap, Lydia leaned back and told me, "I can't believe you brought a total stranger home to dinner. Where's Marco? I think Pasha chased him off. I must say I love being in a real home with animals and cookbooks and furniture! Everything I'd sell my soul for."

"I'm so happy you're here. Unless, of course, you're Jackie the Ripper. Marco's in his little basket. He knows enough to give Pasha what he wants. Pasha is the alpha male around here."

Lydia laughed.

"Hardly Jackie the Ripper, I'm a dull, well-bred English writer."

"What kind of writer? I've always wanted to write."

"I started out in theater, did some acting, then directing, and then I went to film school. I'm writing a thriller now with a lot of new-age themes. I'm really at yoga under false pretenses, I'm doing research, but I think there's something to this breathing thing."

"I bet you're a terrific writer. It's obvious you're a witch too, because Pasha never does that with strangers. I don't even remember the last time he slept in my lap."

"What does your husband do?"

"He's a cameraman."

"Right up my alley. I'm divorced."

"You don't seem old enough to be divorced. But of course, I was a child bride myself. A pregnant child bride, I might add."

Lydia smiled. "I'd love to meet your boys. I'd love to have boys of my own. There's someone unsuitable in the picture. I seem to specialize in unsuitable and unavailable."

He's probably married, I thought. And almost asked her.

Marco jumped up from his basket and began to yip excitedly. In another minute Jules was in the kitchen and Marco had jumped into his arms.

"Home early! Jules, this is my friend Lydia. Lydia's a screenwriter. We met at yoga."

Jules set Marco down. Then went to the sink to wash, wash, wash. And use his usual half a roll of paper towels to dry his hands. And not any old paper towels, he insisted on the Jules super-expensive brand that cost $1.50 per roll. Starving children, homeless women, I was in the habit of berating myself for denying them and providing Jules with his wasteful paper habit that he refused to let me substitute with plain white cloth towels.

When he sat down at the table he smiled at Lydia. "Ah, an old soul like Harriet."

Then Jules put his hands in front of his heart and said in his best Indian accent, "Berry pleased to meet you."

Lydia too was good with an accent. "And I'm berry, berry pleased to meet you as well."

I can see myself so clearly that evening, bustling around as I always did, comfortable in front of this beautiful stranger, serving my husband, serving her.

"Ah mung!" intoned Jules. "'Tis a good wife who makes her husband and master a plate of mung."

Lydia was laughing. I was laughing. Nothing Jules likes better than a peanut gallery laughing at his cuteness.

I served Lydia her fruit salad and she made some ecstatic noises. This time in her normal, charming English accent.

"Fruit salad with mint. What a lucky man you are Jules!"

Yes, right away it felt good having Lydia around. She fit in seamlessly between Jules and me, smoothing out all our differences, bringing out a better us while she was present.

Though Jules, being Jules, afterward had to say, "Do you think she lays it on with the accent? Those limeys get away with murder. The accent fools everybody into thinking they're smarter than we are. In fact, when some of the stupidest people out there are Brits."

I rolled my eyes in the mirror, patted on some face cream and eye cream and lifted up my face a bit in my hands. I was thinking of buying some of those things called "Frownies" that are really just tape to hold up the flesh of your face. Gloria Swanson wore them in *Sunset Boulevard* when William Holden wasn't around. One of the techies at the studio with a very tight jaw was always talking about the stuff, touting its virtues.

Jules was inside his closet.

"Besides, I don't trust those spiritual types."

"She's not one of those spiritual types. She's at yoga doing research on a script that's set among a spiritual sect. She tutors rich kids and writes greeting cards for money. Imagine someone with her education tutoring and writing greeting cards."

"I noticed she worked in the Cambridge thing right away. Everyone who went to Harvard has to tell you they went to Harvard right away. Usually it's in the first five seconds. 'Hello, I went to Harvard.' She—what's her name—at least showed a little restraint and waited twenty minutes. I liked her in fact."

"Me too. I like her better than anyone I've met in a long time, actually. I also like the fact that her boobs are big, but they're real. She may have the only set of real boobs on the West Side of Los Angeles. You go to yoga and during *savasanah* the floor looks like a small mountain range in spandex."

Jules could be counted on never to laugh at my jokes, though I thought this one might have merited a "very cute, Harriet," his version of a rave. I've taken an informal poll over the years and have concluded that there aren't very many husbands who do in fact laugh at their wives' jokes. Lisa, who could rouse a corpse with her wisecracks, says it's the same at her house. And so does Susan, who is brilliant and sarcastic, my two personal favorites. My friend Arianna, who is also hilarious, claims she has never once merited a titter from Bob.

Jules, still in his closet, wasn't tittering either.

"I hadn't noticed," he said at last.

But, he *had* noticed. I had seen my husband eyeing her rack when he thought I was serving fruit salad.

Just for the record: I had never thought much about racks (unless they were lamb) until lately when Jules began to ask me how come I always wore the flattening kind of sports bra. And couldn't I get one with a little something to lift them up?

I was more than a little surprised.

"You never told me you were a boob man. I

thought you liked legs!"

"Legs are good," he replied, but didn't mention mine, which are pretty good if I do say so myself.

But my feelings were a little hurt about the boobs; I've always liked mine, which are small and unassuming. And I thought Jules liked them too. And I was thinking about getting some new kind of sports bra with a little padding built in.

Jules walked out of the closet and came to the edge of the bed where he sat down.

"She's a nice girl, Harriet. But don't go giving it all away."

Was Jules warning me, even that first night, that Lydia was trouble?

"I don't know what you're talking about!" I replied.

And truly, I didn't. But I was already planning on the next time I'd have her to dinner.

Five

I'M NOT GOING TO MISS MY LITTLE DUMP IN WEST LA. I call it "the cottage cheese plate" because of the ceiling and because the place is so bland and blah. The kitchen is atrocious. The appliances are brown, the Formica counters (and how I hate Formica) are avocado colored and chipped, and there's no place to put anything inside or out. Not that I have anything here.

How different from Healthy Harriet's home kitchen with its old oak table and Shaker chairs, the gleaming stainless-steel six-burner Viking, the stately Sub-Zero, and the All-Clad and French copper pots hanging from a round rack on the ceiling. And my knives, how I miss my stainless-steel chef's knives, my paring knives in carbon steel, my bread knife, my cheese knives. Because I wanted a clean slate, I only took one: the small Global Sam gave me that I treasure above all knives, and of course, a sharpening stone. I'm beginning to think it's true about this feng shui business. I'm relieved to be getting rid of the clutter of the old life and starting out new. Which is what I plan to do when I get out of here. And that's soon. Thank the Goddess I have a job.

Obviously I'm taking as much money as I can get. Jules is being very gracious about money, given who he is. I don't mean generous, I don't even mean fair, but he could have played much harder ball, because I did sign an iron-clad prenup drawn up by his mother's white-glove law firm—and I could have ended up with almost nothing. I'm thinking this is Lydia's gracious influence. Though she took my husband and my home, she isn't the type to begrudge me a few bucks.

I'm taking the sentimental stuff: my pictures of the boys at whatever stage Jules deigned to photograph them (a prime example of the shoemaker's shoeless children); we have remarkably few pictures of any of us given that Jules used to be a still photographer. I've got my good pictures of Marco on my phone. I took my grandmother's strongbox out of the house and my beautiful old rug I bought when I signed *Healthy Harriet*'s cable show. It's been sitting at the rug cleaners since I dumped it there when I moved out. I took Dan's favorite bear, whom he called Daffodil Jones, and I'm embarrassed to say it's

Daffodil I take to bed with me at the cottage cheese plate. Dan would hate that! And I'm certain he would toss Daffodil Jones in the nearest garbage bin. I put the stuff in storage that the boys said they might want, which wasn't much, and I left Jules and Lydia the rest. Lydia should have the good sense to buy furniture she likes now, when she has a little clout. Jules doesn't like new things and hates spending money. Perhaps he'll be a new man with Lydia, although I doubt it.

I've probably been playing the guilt card since the day I walked out the door, fighting fire with fire. Though I'm sure if my boys, one of them or both of them, had been around, I wouldn't have gone so far. I'm still worried about traumatizing them. I'm glad they won't see the cottage cheese plate.

When I get to New York, I look forward to having things again: living room furniture, new knives, I'll probably get some kind of pet, and one by one the pots and skillets that have always sustained me. The twins will come and visit and we'll have some meals at home and life will return to normal. The New Normal, I hope.

The real questions remains: will the end of my time here mean the end of feeling guilty? I hope so. It's hardly brain surgery to figure out what's been going on. Old Harriet has been bent over with guilt ... this Spartan existence, her version of a hair shirt so she doesn't have to feel guilty for running away from Jules, taking all the money she can get, and leaving the old life behind. But getting rid of guilt isn't just a matter of declaring, "Out, out, damn guilt!" Like exercise, guilt is something that works its way inside the muscles and bloodstream. Guilt is a habit of mind just like exercise is a habit of body. And of course Jules, more than anyone else, always made me feel guilty. That was his singular power over me. One that, in the end, I turned on him. By that point, he was dying for Lydia, who in turn refused to float in a sea of morally ambiguous indefinitely; she was in a terrible bind, poor girl, and needed the security of solid ground beneath her feet. Caught between her feelings for me (it sounds weird, but we really liked each other) and the natural desire for a house, a husband . . . and a baby. Jules could have gone either way, though obviously he was at a dangerous age, he wanted that young flesh so he'd feel young again himself. It's the old theme and variation of the vampire.

He did try to keep us both, Lydia and me, without disrupting his life or the private income too much. It was touch and go for awhile with all of us living there together . . . myself, I nearly broke from the pressure. The main thing is, in the end, we all got what we wanted: everybody won. That's why the whole thing was very tricky. When you are Jules, nobody else is allowed to win.

I just got back from getting my hair streaked and blown straight . . . a hundred and fifty bucks, plus tip, which is "nothing!" according to my friend Arianna who pays three fifty to some joint in Beverly Hills. If I go to yoga tonight, and do the usual amount of sweating, I'll take a shower afterward and my new fashionable do that took forty minutes with a blow dryer to create will be down the drain. When my friends do this sort of thing I say, "You look fabulous!" and secretly think, *Harriet, don't you fall for this enslavement shit*. It can't be an accident that today, when women are doing so well economically, our beauty regimes—meant to make us look so free and natural—are in reality keeping us at the gym and the beauty salon for longer hours than ever before. The hair rollers and girdles of the older generation were actually nothing compared to what women go through now with the blow dryer and the grueling exercise, the straight, streaked hair and all this endless waxing, perfect eyebrows, power peels, the list goes on and on.

God knows I've never aspired to the mother-earth look, I came of age prior to leave-in hair products and before everybody had these teeth the color of printer paper, myself included.

THE NEW ME

When I was growing up, mothers wore foundation garments and we didn't wear bras. Now, when you're forty you're supposed to look like something out of the Victoria's Secret catalog... a lioness in a push-up bra and waist string. In fact, you're only allowed to look forty at sixty-five or seventy. Though honestly, it seems to me we're all starting to look exactly the same.

As for Jules, Lydia, and me, why, we all won ... yes, even little old me, and that's my private cross to bear, having gotten what I wanted and certainly what I deserved. It's odd, how it's something I've never read about, but I know it must go on, this guilt thing that isn't exactly fear of success as much as guilt at succeeding. And not in the sense that I don't deserve this, but, in my case anyway, if I get used to this, someone will take it away or even kill me. Yes, small and unthreatening though they were, my desires frightened the hell out of me—never mind Jules who was in the habit of nipping the smallest one in the bud. Why did I give him so much power? I have no idea, except that I was as uncomfortable about having power as he was in my having it. That was one of the few things we absolutely agreed on.

Take Thanksgiving, the only holiday I really care about. If Jules was on location (which he was for the first years of the boys' lives at holiday times) we always had to go to him; even though there were three of us, he would be on hiatus, I was working my hardest during the holidays, and the boys were often sick during that time as children are.

Being Jules, he would never be upfront with his plans. Withholding vital information pertaining to family life was the chief way he had of keeping the troops at home under control. Everything was a shocking *fait accompli*. I wouldn't know he was going on location until the very last second. One minute he'd be shooting a string of very lucrative commercials in New York, and the next moment we'd be standing in front of our apartment, Dan holding one hand and Sam the other, waving him off, his cab filled with suitcases. Then he would be off to Canada, or Texas, or Georgia, the Philippines, or wherever the movie was going to be shot, which never seemed to be New York.

"Daddy's going again?" the boys would say before he left.

"You'll be home for Thanksgiving, won't you?" I'd pipe in.

And Jules would begin by replying, "Of course! It's the worst time to travel, but I wouldn't do that to you and the boys."

"Good!"

Then he'd take the boys for carriage rides in Central Park, and out to fancy lunches with just the three of them. And balloons, he'd always send dozens of helium balloons to the boys the day he left. They'd drift around the ceiling like lost souls for days after.

Me, I didn't get much special treatment unless we were fighting when he left, then I'd get some flowers. Though sex in those days was so good, who cared?

When I'd bring up Thanksgiving again, the night before he was leaving, he'd say, "You know Harriet, maybe we should mix Thanksgiving up this year. It would be great to miss the fucking parade, for once. I started going with Freeman alone when I was around their age."

"Jules, they're five years old. Your mother is nuts; you know that. Honestly, I don't know how the two of you survived. Besides, the boys love the parade. I love it too. You native New Yorkers are so blasé. If you want, I can take them and you can baste."

"I'll just forget and the turkey will be dry. God, I hate Thanksgiving! It's only September, and it makes me nuts thinking of it."

"I love Thanksgiving. It's actually the only holiday I really like. And Lisa will be here this year. I already invited her."

"I hate Thanksgiving."

"I hate Christmas."

"You're the only Jew I know who doesn't like Christmas."

"Do you really like it?"

"I don't know. Sort of."

By this point, I would be feeling guilty, thinking I had deprived Jules and the boys of the happiness and sense of belonging assimilated Jews enjoy when they celebrate the gentile holidays, just as if we too were card-carrying members of the white people's club.

"Jules," I'd say, "do you want us to celebrate Christmas?"

"It's too late. It's not our tradition, but it would have been nice."

Dan also complained that all the other Jews in his kindergarten class had Christmas trees, so why didn't we?

Then when Dan started hating me, I felt guilty, thinking I should have given him a Christmas tree; I should have made some Easter baskets. Why was I always such a ridiculous pain in the ass about things that didn't matter to me? I could care less about the Jewish thing. Except if someone says something anti-Semitic, and then I care a lot.

"So when are you leaving?"

"Maybe day after tomorrow, I don't really know."

"No way, Jules!"

"Principal photography starts in three weeks. It's a low-budgie, so there's not a lot of preproduction, but I need to scout locations and get crew, thank God I'm getting per diem."

"Is it union?"

"Yeah, I think so."

"If this winter's anything like last year, we'll save thousands. God, I hope the boys' ears grow out of this . . ."

"So what is this, the old guilt trip?"

"No, that's not why I said that."

"You want me to feel guilty because I got a gig in LA. You know eventually we're going to have to move there."

"So, what am I, chopped liver?"

"No you're sushi. High-grade sushi. Come here . . ."

And so we'd lay there for a while, Jules and me, fooling around; we did a lot of fooling around back then.

Often I'd playfully ask, "Jules do you cheat on me?"

"Every minute of every day."

"What about those tall skinny jeans I found in your stuff, you've still never explained about them."

"They were mine."

"You haven't ever been that skinny."

"I lose weight when I'm on location. Maybe they got mixed in at the fluff and fold."

"You've never gone to a fluff and fold in your life."

"You used to send out stuff to the fluff and

fold. It gave me a rash with that detergent."

"So who was she?"

"Who?"

"The tall skinny-jeans girl?"

"You're out of your mind, Harriet."

"God, you won't even be here for Halloween."

"Christ, I suppose you love Halloween too!"

"If you'd grown up in Murpheysfield, Louisiana you'd love Halloween in New York. You'd love all the New York holidays."

"St. Patrick's Day?"

"St. Patrick's day is gross. I'll give you that . . ."

"So how come you don't like Christmas? Christmas in New York is great."

"Christmas depresses me. I don't like the food either."

"You also hate potato latkes."

"True, but I like the applesauce. How come you're changing the subject again when I'm trying to pour out my heart?"

"Huh?"

"C'mere."

Afterward, he'd say, "Maybe you and the boys should come to LA for Thanksgiving. You can get away from the cold."

"What about Lisa and everybody else I invited? What about all my clients?"

"I'll be dead tired, Harriet, this movie means

so much to me."

I was dead tired too and at that moment, totally fucked out.

"Okay. So we'll come to LA. I'll tell Lisa she can join us in LA."

"Harriet, you're an angel," Jules would say, and that would be my reward.

Luckily for me, LA really worked out well for my career. Once I got over the initial shock (one that lasted more than year), I was okay. I made friends, so did the boys (me with ex-New Yorkers, the boys oftentimes with children of ex-New Yorkers; birds of a feather, as they say). The funny thing about LA, at least the LA I lived in, is that whenever we would end up at a party it was always with ex-New Yorkers who would spend the whole time frantically demanding of each other, "And where did you live?"

"What year did you move, '98? We moved in '99."

"We were bicoastal until 2000."

People talked about the apartments they left behind, "a huge two bedroom with maid's quarters on West End, worth a fortune in today's market. I was three blocks from Fairway."

"I was two blocks from Zabars . . ."

"We were around the corner from Balducci's, but thank God we sublet; we're going back before we kill ourselves."

"We lived in Chinatown when it was still affordable."

As for Jules and me, we never owned an apartment in New York because Jules always refused to buy a three bedroom, or a two bedroom, or really anything; we always rented.

But we eventually bought a house in LA because the kind of food I do (healthy, vegetable-oriented, non-fussy food) turned out to be perfect there. I started out doing the home cooking bit where you prepare a day's or week's worth of food for microwaving. I began with just main dishes. Though in the end, I had my pretty HH label, which looked like something from Her Royal Majesty's pantry, on everything from prewashed baby greens to bottles of olive oil and balsamic mixed together with a few herbs and sold for a huge markup.

I discovered that as long as you made it tasty with a good-looking label, you could charge a fortune. Then when the healthy food kick started the fortune turned into a king's ransom, at least in food terms. I was always pinching myself, wondering how I could have gotten so lucky. I gave my leftovers to a food bank, I sent contributions to soup kitchens in my area, and I worked my ass off. Which is why, after several years, when they offered me the cable show, I was glad to take it. Because truthfully, I was dead tired and ready to do something else. My clients were the families who didn't have a cook, though they had every other kind of helper. People in LA, especially the film-industry crowd, want healthy food. I've even noticed lately that the psychologists are jumping on the eat-dinner-together bandwagon. Healthy Harriet promised no unhealthy oils, and minimal sugar. If I used butter, I did so very sparingly. Eventually, when I added desserts (an ex-hippie in Topanga baked for me) I was very careful about the trans-fat thing. And I only offered fresh-fruit pies made with seasonal fruit. I also had staple items such as applesauce (my biggest seller), turkey chili, and each week a different kind of soup. I would make a hearty one, often with beans, in the cooler months, and a refrigerated light one in the summer. These I sold in plastic one-quart containers apart from my dinners.

Anyway, I caught on very quickly. Friends told their friends about me, and soon I had a Viking, then two Vikings and a Sub-Zero in the kitchen as well as several adjunct refrigerators. I had assistants from the Culinary Institute, and in time, a student from UCLA who delivered for me ... not to mention a half-dozen other cooks on the payroll, Valentina as my Girl Friday, and someone at the nearby farmers' market—all of whom did their thing and sent it out under my label. We had a great time. And unlike most working mothers, I got to be there when the boys came home from school. In fact, it was Dan who came up with Healthy Harriet's name. "I'm sick of Healthy Harriet, can't we have something else?"

What was the secret of my success? A lot of ambitious food people were turning out tasty, healthy food for the trendy, skinny people and their trendy, skinny families in my neck of the woods, which ran roughly from the ocean to a little beyond Barrington in Brentwood; a street of boring condos and suburban-type restaurants and shops made famous by OJ and his motley crew.

My claim to fame was HH's half-whole-wheat biscuits. Granted they had calories galore, especially if you put butter and honey on them, still they were healthier than your basic white-flour biscuits being made with whole-wheat flour, which browns very nicely too. HH's half-whole-wheat biscuits were golden and crunchy on the outside and soft on the inside, and I sent them gratis with every order. Depending on the meal plan, this could be up to a dozen per family.

People are finally demanding good bread in LA and getting it, I'm glad to say, though LA will never be New York bread-wise. When I first started coming to LA in my early twenties, visiting Jules on location, the bread situation was hopeless. For the record, I can't stand biscuits and wouldn't eat one, even if biscuits didn't make you fat—and mine are better in all ways than the Gold Medal/Crisco version I learned to make in Murpheysfield, Louisiana—biscuits will always remind me of the South; therefore, forget about eating them. Apparently, no one else feels as I do because at the end of my home-cooking thing, I had a side business going on with HH's half-whole-wheat biscuits that amazed even Jules. I had to rent commercial space and kept two full-time ladies very busy baking biscuits. Back before I took the cable show, I had a couple of offers to buy the name and I curse myself daily for not striking when the iron was hot, because I had my twenty minutes of HH-biscuit fame and now my name is worth nothing.

Maybe when I go back, I'll try the biscuits in New York, though somehow, I can't imagine them having the same impact they did with the Santa Monica/Brentwood crowd. I was sending HH's half-whole-wheat biscuits out at the height of the protein diet craze, which was probably why they were such a hit, being forbidden fruit and all.

If LA turned out well for me money-wise, it didn't turn out to be the career boon Jules had expected. He got better gigs when he was going back and forth between New York and LA. Once we moved here, he went from shooting "A" features to "B" features to eventually landing in series TV. Though Jules was always bringing home very good bacon and has inherited money besides, I knew his heart wasn't really in the mediocre crap he was working on. That he wasn't getting the work he was meant to. And some of that had to do with my doing so well. At least that's the way it always played itself out.

I also know that had I been in some other sort of business, I never could have succeeded the same way I did in food. Food, like literature, is one of the few areas in which a woman can have a family and get away with being successful for the simple reason that plying the trade doesn't create too much resistance around the house. In the case of literature, women novelists have always been able to sneak in a few pages while no one was looking, with or without rooms of their own. Food is even more subversive, because under the guise of feeding and nurturing the cook is doing what she wants, too. Some of us even manage to make a good living.

In my case, my love affair with cooking started very early. I remember the first time I successfully made bolognaise (the Anglo way with butter, green pepper, onion, hamburger meat, garlic salt, white sugar, tomato paste, and a big can of American tomatoes) standing on a stool in my mother's kitchen one Thursday, it being Noog's day off. Noog was my mother's house-keeper whom I adored and who adored me.

Noog taught me how to cook. She also taught me that someone could love me. I was her pet, her baby girl; it was a mutual lovefest. When she died some years ago, I felt the way people do when their beloved mothers die.

But that long ago day, standing on the stool in my real mother's kitchen, I remember ten-tatively dipping my spoon in the bright acidic mixture, removing a dollop to a small bowl, sprinkling it with that fake Kraft shit (the only cheese I knew about other than Velveeta) the stuff that still comes in the green foil cylinder. Finally, the triumphant taste of my success. Not even Mother striding in moments later, full of scotch and pissed off from her losses at bridge, red lacquer nails poised with a smoking Marl-boro, and screaming at me at the top of her hoarse voice for messing up the kitchen on Noog's day off could take away from it. Or, that from then on, cooking would be my foundation for happiness.

I don't mind baking. But, real food has always been my passion, though in the past few years I've given up eating meat, I still cook it for my family and my show. Since I don't have for-mal training, I have, to this day, never dealt with a whole dead bird when you have to gut it and pluck it and singe off the feathers. Under Jules' guidance, I have cleaned a few fish, gagging as I did so. But I still eat fish, so I must not have gotten all that grossed out.

Once in a while, like on Thanksgiving, I eat a little white meat, but I don't feel good about it. I keep promising myself to go to Chinatown in New York or LA, pick out some poor, pathetic chicken, and watch it being killed, but I haven't worked up the strength. I'm chicken, I suppose, though strangely enough my toleration for eating birds does not extend to ducks. I wouldn't eat a duck (or prepare one) no matter how much you paid me. With duck, like pig or lamb or cow, I have no trouble imagining the *quack quack* of its suffering.

When I move back to New York and set up my new kitchen, I'm hoping to make just high-end, trendy vegetarian food and thus make my new kitchen free from any creature's blood. Honestly, I look forward to making dinner again; it's been a long while, the idea being to wean myself away from doing anything domestic.

I allow myself to go out and eat with friends several nights a week. And I'm allowed to go on dates involving a main course, provided I don't prepare or serve the entrée. Cooking dinners for friends in their kitchens, or earning money as a chef in someone else's house (something I do once in a while because it pays really well), is also okay.

Since mornings and nights are still nippy, I've taken to making yam fries in the toaster oven here at the cottage cheese plate. The Healthy Harriet way is to slice a yam into medallions, brush with oil, and slam at 400° until crisp. Right before they're done, sprinkle with cinnamon and slam that on the toaster setting to crisp them up. Easy and yummy! I have this for dinner all the time. With a little steamed broccoli, it's a perfect meal.

If I'm not going out at night, I'll eat a late lunch, go to yoga, and come home for some fruit or a salad. If I'm cold, soup, as long as the soup is not homemade. Because, for me anyway, love begins and ends with dinner. Until I can be sure I'm cooking for a gem and not Jules all over again, I'm going to play it safe and stay away from dinner, and that's that.

Some days I wake up in the tacky cottage cheese plate in West LA, husbandless, with only Dan's teddy bear to keep me company, my boys so far away, and I can't imagine how this has come to pass. Who was I kidding? Was I crazy letting Lydia into our lives like that? Still, getting away from Jules and having been marooned for a time at this vacant place has something to do with my old dreams, I think. I've been trying to remember what they were these past months... I've been thinking about them anyway.

Six

I LOOKED FOR LYDIA THE NEXT FEW DAYS AT YOGA, hoping to see her, but no raven-haired Anglo-Saxon beauties appeared beside me. The classes were filled as usual with the California bleach blondes with mountain ranges on their chests.

It was at the Wednesday farmers' market where we met again.

It had been a particularly grueling morning Jules-wise. He had cut himself shaving and that always throws him into a tizzy.

Just in from a run with Marco, who was proving to be the best running buddy ever, I found my husband fulminating in the kitchen with a wad of toilet paper hanging off his chin.

"We're out of Band-Aids. And alcohol and hydrogen peroxide and you've forgotten Neosporin for months. I cut myself and there was nothing to put on it."

"I'm sorry you cut yourself," I said, trying

to be sympathetic. I wasn't feeling particularly sympathetic. "I'll put it on the list, Jules."

By this time, Marco was jumping up and down and yipping. Just like Jules, he always got excited when Jules went at it. Too bad the big terrier wasn't as cheerful as the little one.

"And get one of those pencil things to staunch the blood. It looks like Friday the thirteenth in our bathroom. I didn't really have time to clean up the blood. I'd rather you—not Valentina—do it. She never washes her hands."

Of course I wouldn't leave a bloody bathroom for Valentina to deal with. Nor did I bother to ask Jules why Valentina cleaning up the blood required sanitized hands. Hydrogen peroxide . . . how could I be out of it? How could I be out of anything on *The List?*

Truthfully, I'd become aware only in the past few years that there actually was an ongoing list that I was supposed to be tending to. Let me state that in another way. Every household has the list that one or the other does. But in our household, I believed that "my list from Jules" was sacrosanct. I believed it as much as he did. It never would have occurred to me to say, "Get it yourself, dickhead." Or in a more polite manner, "Could you pick up this or that on your way home from work, darling?"

Marco too, unfortunately, had added momentum to the list making. Not that I minded anything having to do with Marco.

"Are you sure you're up to date with his rabies shots?"

"Yes, dear."

"How about the stuff for ticks. There's an epidemic of tick-related illnesses in animals. I heard about it on the radio coming home. I also think you need to get him one of those implants in case he runs away."

"I'm going to do that when I get him altered."

"Altered?" Jules said with disgust. "I hate that word. Why don't people just say the truth, 'cut off their balls!' And while we're on the subject, why do you have to cut his balls off? Just because some PC assholes from the Nanny State claim it's the right thing to do—never mind the vet lobby. How much do they charge for cutting off balls?"

"I haven't asked yet. I just assumed we'd do it—you're supposed to do it before the dog is a year old."

"Don't even think about doing it without consulting me."

"Fine, Jules."

Marco jumped up as terriers do, yipping cheerfully.

"See, he knows I'm defending him, don't you Marco?"

At the farmers' market, I was behind some old man in the line for baby lettuces, one who was involved in a huge, entirely unnecessary fight with the sweet, passive-aggressive back-to-earth kids who grew and sold the best baby lettuces I'd ever had.

Apparently they weren't paying attention to him and took someone else before they took him.

The old man began to wag his finger. I studied his profile, which looked like an older saggy version of Jules with the strong aquiline nose and the perfect chin, and I felt like I was looking through a window into my future.

"I've been waiting here for five minutes. You took three people before you took me."

The kid who handled the cash was probably stoned, now that I think of it. He nodded his head absently.

"Chill out dude, what will you have?"

This set the old guy off again, and I decided to forgo the best baby lettuce in the market. Second or third best would do just fine.

When I whirled around, that's when I saw her: tall, black-haired Lydia dressed all in white. She looked like a gorgeous flapper with her sleek, shining hair and long legs.

"Harriet, what luck running into you!"

We hugged briefly.

"It's wonderful, isn't it? Two seconds ago we didn't know the other one existed and now we're in each other's lives. Do you ever think about the randomness of the cosmos, do you think it's all karma?"

Lydia looked at me as though I'd said something very interesting and profound.

"I'm on the fence. I'm attracted to the spiritual side, but I'm skeptical too. I was educated to question. Learnt it at my daddy's knee."

She gestured to my four-tiered shopping cart filled with the early fall harvest. Tomatoes, peppers, potatoes, there were even still late-season peaches and strawberries. A couple of my favorite vendors called out to me. I bumped into some people I knew and introduced Lydia. After all, this was my métier.

Lydia carried an attractive basket. It dangled from her beautifully shaped arm like a fashion accessory, not a shopping tool.

"Are you working today?"

"I'm tutoring late this afternoon. I'm a bit stuck with the screenplay. I'm afraid it's just crap."

"I can't see you writing anything that isn't really good. You're so authentic. I'm sure your writing is too. I'd love to read some."

"Be careful what you wish for, Harriet."

"Why don't you come home with me for lunch?"

"You just had me for dinner."

"Feeding people is my life," I told her truthfully. "But just so you know, I'm very picky about who I ask to feed. I'd love your company. You'd be doing me a favor."

Then I told her what we were going to have.

"I made corn salad, roasted beets and faro with feta and radicchio. I'm testing out new things."

"How can I say no to that, Harriet?"

Our cars were parked near each other and when we got to mine first, Lydia helped me load my shopping in.

"Do you remember where I live?" I asked.

"It's seared in my memory!"

I'd come back to that "seared" from time to time when the whole thing started unraveling, but that day I was charmed by her speaking to me in literary cook speak.

When I pulled up to my white two-story Spanish in the North of Wilshire neighborhood, she had already beaten me there.

Just like before, Pasha went right to Lydia, circling her ankles. Marco tried to jump into her lap.

"I'm glad this is your second time here. The first time a new friend comes home it's like that first day of school, so scary!"

Lydia laughed. "Maybe you should write a funny, healthy cookbook."

"That's such a nice thought. I was offered this job recently in New York and part of the job is to put out some big report. Though I don't think it is meant to be a funny report."

"Are you going to accept? I'd adore New York. Other than the weather, it's much more my style."

"Me, too. I didn't exactly formally turn down the job. But Jules doesn't want us to do the bicoastal thing. We did almost five years of it. It was pretty exhausting. He'll have to change his mind if my show is replaced with *Trevor Teen Gourmand*."

"Is there any possibility of that?"

"There's always a possibility when you're not a name brand. It's funny, I can almost see old Trevor with his plate of white truffles ... he's very snotty, my Trevor."

"Ah yes," laughed Lydia. "And I'll have to tutor him."

Valentina, who had been upstairs cleaning, came into the kitchen then. I asked her if she had eaten, and told her to get a plate and sit down with us.

Valentina was oddly formal and declined. The cat jumped down off Lydia's lap and disappeared into another part of the house. Valentina and the cat didn't get on. I never figured out which one instigated the animosity, but it was mutual by now and well entrenched.

Something of that ill feeling seemed to have replaced the light-hearted atmosphere of the room just moments before. Lydia announced she needed to go home to work and left.

"Isn't she pretty?" I enthused after she had gone.

Valentina was at the kitchen sink by then. Maybe the water running kept her from hearing me or maybe she wasn't answering. Right away, Valentina, normally so warm and friendly (except to Pasha and to Jules) was manifestly cool about my new friend. Was it that obvious from the get-go that a New Me was in the offing?

Furthermore, did I know what I was doing when I asked Lydia to take care of Marco while I was in New York for parents' day at NYU?

In retrospect, it's easy to say, I must have known on some level—just as Valentina knew on some level—Lydia was trouble. I was acting as if I knew. Acting out of what the psychologists call "middle knowledge" and I'm guessing I did and I didn't. What I knew absolutely is that I would never have the wherewithal to leave Jules all on my own. I'd thought about it off and on for years, even gone as far as consulting a lawyer and I was thinking about it now. But, I never could imagine the big scene where I said, "I'm outta here."

Still manifestly, it must have been on my

mind. Why else did I enlist my new friend to take care of Marco when I was in New York when I could just as easily have had Valentina take him home? I was pissed off of course that Jules refused to come with me to parents' day, claiming he was too busy to even look after Marco. Being Jules, he announced the no-show plan the night before air time, when I had to get up at four the next morning.

"There isn't a thing I can do, Harriet. I'll call my mom and explain. I'll be lucky if I can even get home to sleep. Are you sure it's not Dan's next week? I'm positive I put it down as Dan's. When did you say the next one was?"

"Next weekend."

"There may be a conflict there too. I won't know until the last minute. It's out of my control."

"You mean you won't take responsibility for your never being there. Are you gonna send them the money you didn't spend on airfare and restaurants?"

"No, they're getting plenty of money. You're always indulging them, Harriet, indulging them and being hostile to me."

"Anytime I call you on your shit, you tell me I'm being hostile. I'm disappointed and the boys will be too. Not to mention your mother."

"Where are you going?"

"To get a sleeping pill."

"You act like a zombie when you take those pills. You even snore. Aren't you supposed to be into healthy living?"

I grabbed Marco and left the room.

From the bed, Jules rang out, "Won't you come home, little Harriet, won't you come home . . ."

Whenever Jules sang in his poignant, off-key way, I was invariably charmed. Why, I don't know, except that love is an idiopathic form of insanity. I should have just felt manipulated, which I did a bit, though not enough to just stay away. I returned, put Marco in his basket, and got back in bed.

Jules turned out his light and our room was dark. I heard him sigh. "Aren't you going to wash your hands after touching the dog?"

The next morning, bleary-eyed, I got in my Volvo and drove to the studio. Deborah, who did my makeup, commented that she hoped I had a good time the night before.

I was exhausted. Nevertheless, it was one of my best shows. And I more or less winged it.

"Today we're going to talk about substitution. The oldest trick in the cook's book. Don't have any pine nuts for your pesto? Use walnuts. They're healthier! I've been cooking since I was young enough to stand on a stool, so I've substituted just about everything for something else.

"In fact, I woke up in the middle of the

night, looked over at Jules, and thought, *Why, if I substituted someone else for me, would he even notice?* I mean as long as the food was good and my substitute laughed at his jokes."

My peanut gallery got a good laugh out of this show, and once more I got some encouraging remarks on our Facebook page.

Clearly a change was in the air whether I was aware of it or not.

Lydia lived in a garage apartment of one of the huge houses north of San Vicente in Santa Monica. The real estate people are always talking about the North of Wilshire and North of Montana demarcations. We lived in North of Wilshire and many of my old Healthy Harriet customers lived in North of Montana. But the real bucks, the kind with their own staffs, lived north of San Vicente. Houses just don't lose their value in that small neck of the very elite woods, recession or no recession.

Three small men with leaf blowers were tending the grass of the huge sprawling hacienda—one that had nary a single stray leaf gracing its very green, all-too-manicured surface. It looked more like a pool table than a front lawn. Fumes were rising up, filling the air with the familiar stench of gasoline. Marco began to bark his head off as he always did when he saw men using leaf blowers. I tightened up his leash, told him to be a good boy, and put my other hand over my nose and mouth because I too hated leaf blowers. Though as always, I felt guilty about the men who were wielding them and tried to make the usual futile gesture to indicate that it wasn't them that stank.

Lydia had been to the house a few days before so I could prep her on the care and feeding of Marco. I had given her the freezer bags containing packets of his homemade dog food and also little plastic bags of his special organic kibble. And of course lots of Healthy Harriet baked treats that had chicken bouillon, oats, blueberries, maple syrup, and human-grade bone meal.

Marco and I passed by the side of the house as a stern-looking blond in a tennis dress and jewelry came out of the front door, heading toward the leaf-blowing trio. I indicated that I was heading to the back and the blond inclined her head to show that she understood. I've been in the food business long enough to know when I can act like a person and when it's appropriate for me to act like a servant. Servants don't enter with pedigree dogs on a leash (unless the dog belongs to the owner), but I did my best to convey in body language that I belonged to the servant class and knew my place. And Marco, being the genius of sensitivity that he was, had already quieted down. Still, I was uneasy. I didn't want to get Lydia in trouble.

We headed up the steps, my darling dog and I; it was always so much fun going anywhere with Marco, who had the cutest little walk. He had the habit of turning to catch my eye and yip when he was walking on his leash. And, of course he was always excited and happy to be anywhere, doing anything. I knocked on Lydia's door. Soon we were in her little kitchen with its cracked sink and worn linoleum on the floor. The kitchen window had one of those *I Love Lucy* kinds of ruffled curtains but the ruffle had lost its life some decades ago. It was actually a pretty charming place compared to the cottage cheese plate, but back then, it looked sort of sad and depressing to me.

Lydia herself didn't look all that happy either.

"Is everything okay?" I asked her. "I don't want to get you in trouble."

"You don't have to worry about me getting in trouble, because the trouble already happened."

"What do you mean?"

"The lady of this manor seemed to think it was perfectly fair to add floors and toilets to my tutoring duties since her last three household slaves quit and she needs help."

"The bleach blond with the tennis dress?"

"And don't forget her tennis bracelets!"

We both laughed.

"Fuck her!" I said, in true Jules style. "She's a lowlife moron."

"Be that as it may, rents in this part of town come dear. Any part of town, come to that."

"How long have you got?"

"Not long, but it's all right, Harriet."

"Is Marco going to make things worse?"

"It's a done deal, Harriet. Don't worry about me. Have a great time in New York; I'll see you Sunday night or Monday morning. Just text me ahead of time and we'll arrange the pick up."

As I mentioned before, I hadn't thought then about inviting Lydia to move in with us. And I had no idea whatsoever that her watching Marco would give her access to my husband. I wasn't in the habit of thinking that way. It wasn't like me to measure myself against this younger, yes, far more desirable, female. Am I denying my own basest emotions? Was I actually jealous, full of rage and envy? I can't really say, because to this day, these sorts of base, albeit realistic, emotions are buried so deep inside me, I have no access to them.

Besides, I really liked Lydia, maybe I loved her. I know I wanted to help her. And I think she wanted to help me too—never mind that Jules, as usual, got in there with his wants and needs. However, I had given some thought to bringing Freeman, Jules' half brother into the picture. He's a hotshot agent and if he liked Lydia, he could do wonders for her prospects in town. I hadn't yet told Lydia about Freeman, but I was going to, whether Jules got involved or not.

"Look, we'll talk about all this when I get back. I may be able to help you. In the meantime, if you get in any trouble, I've emailed you Valentina's number. And Jules can always be called in a pinch."

I kissed Marco on the top of his silky head and hugged Lydia. A couple of hours later I was in a cab heading to LAX and the afternoon flight into JFK.

PART II

Seven

JULES WAS BORN WITH A SILVER SPOON IN HIS MOUTH, but he was, in every way, a poor and hungry little rich boy. We had that in common, Jules and me. In my case, however, though I experienced almost no real nurturing (except from Noog), unlike Jules there was no moolah to compensate for my suffering. My parents died young and broke. Afterward, my siblings and I walked away from one another, not wanting to revisit our childhoods.

Yes, our mothers were weird. Mine was overly smothering but really rather cold as those smothering, insensitive types can be. Gloria, Jules' mother, was and is just plain cold. Our fathers were effectively nonexistent except for occasional violent appearances. We received any warmth and holding in our early lives from tired arms wearing uniforms. When we married and had the twins in our early twenties, it was the first time either one of us had a real family.

Gloria still lives in a huge apartment on Central Park West, the kind people kill for, and she lives there all alone, not thinking there is anything unusual about wandering around in close to three thousand square feet all by her lonesome. Jules and his half brother Freeman grew up there. Freeman is older and came from an even worse marriage than the one between Jules' father and mother. And the two of them aren't close to each other or to her. If there wasn't a good deal of family money involved, I doubt if either one of them would even speak to her or to each other. As it is, they hardly do. I can't blame them, either.

Family money: another one of the problems at our house. Neither one of us could ever deal with it. For my part, I knew it was there, but I never asked for any of it. It paid for the times when Jules was between gigs, and for summer camp for the boys, musical instruments, COL-LEGE. I never once in all those years steamed open any of the envelopes addressed in Gloria's thin, spidery handwriting. And I signed our joint income taxes without looking or bother-ing to understand what was going on. I found out from my lawyer this is surprisingly common in certain marriages; even when the wife works and contributes her fair share, she still remains completely in the dark. Or in my case, kept herself in the dark.

Gloria never wrote "personal" or "confidential" on the envelopes. She knew Jules well enough to know she didn't have to. My fault or Jules'? Both of course. Jules didn't want to give, I didn't know how to be a big girl and take. We were perfectly meshed in that way. Ultimately, when I was forced recently to really look at the situation, I realized it was just the same old story of the guy shutting the wife out, 1950s' style. But to me, who had been working her ass off all these years, it came as a hard blow. Now, I can see how I fucked up. When the boys were growing up, when I wanted to get them something nice, I didn't consult Jules. I just bought what each one wanted with my own money, knowing on some level the big stuff, the important stuff, would be taken care of. Still, a lot of families operate like this, where one person is the nice parent and the other is the mean one, the difficult one; the one who always says no. But honestly, I don't think it's such a great policy. Nor do I think it was the right way to go, looking back. I should have made Jules toe the line somehow. I should have stood up to him more, both for my sake and the boys. I had nothing to lose except maybe my own view of myself. I always overpaid my babysitters in the early days, my kitchen helpers once the business got going, and spent a lot of energy hiding small things like this from Jules, who for his part hid all the big things from me. And, yes, I always paid my way. I was afraid of him, afraid of the money, because I knew he didn't want me to have it. Or talk about it, or touch it, or enjoy it. Or have any of the things it could buy that were fun. The money was his and his alone and he called all the financial shots. And, because I was proud and wanted to pay my own way, I ended up not saving any of my own money either.

Once in a while, Jerry, our accountant, would call and say, "You're paying your help too much sweetheart. In the name of God we're going broke here." But either Jerry didn't rat me out to Jules or Jules knew and had Jerry speak for him. No one ever gave me trouble as long as I was putting money in the till.

I suppose by nature I'm on the generous side. I love buying presents and giving things to friends and family. And I've always spent exorbitant sums on fresh fruit and vegetables. And good equipment. However, luxury items for myself frighten me. Most of my married years found me wrapped in a chef's apron, big and white, the kind you can bleach. A half a dozen used to hang on a coat hook in the kitchen.

I hope when I go back to New York I will have made some progress in that direction; though, now of course I'm on my own, on a much smaller budget. So I never did work out the money thing between Jules and me. Still—and this is a big still—Jules bought me out of the house and paid me off enough so I can move, set myself up, and put a little away in the bank. I got it almost right away in a lump sum because I knew Jules would never send me alimony checks and would find some way to wiggle out of it. I was holding my breath right up until the check cleared last week. I was grateful, and still am, that I don't have to worry about things like the boys' college tuition. After all, Jules could be just as selfish, just as much a pain in the ass and not have had a private income.

I arrived very late at night at Jules' childhood home. The doorman gave me the key. I could see the pool of light outside of Gloria's bedroom door down the long carpeted hall, one that was hung with many pictures of Gloria back when she was gorgeous, and one or two of Jules and Freeman when they were young and vulnerable; she didn't come out to greet me. By the time I was up and about the next morning, she was already at her exercise class. I hurried and got out of the apartment before she returned.

It had been quite a few years since I was back in New York in the fall. The leaves were just starting to turn and there was a little crispness in the air when I set out across the park, dressed in real clothes and real shoes, not the sneakers and exercise clothes everybody wears in LA. I felt both sophisticated and grown-up in a way I hadn't in a long time.

I was due to meet Sam later on after lunch, but I was looking forward to this first morning on my own. I headed straight to Neue Gallery, my favorite of all places in New York, maybe the world, though I haven't seen too much of the world—that's another thing I plan to do now when I can: travel. The Neue also has fabulous coffee and bread. And if I was remembering correctly, chestnut soup: an Austrian specialty.

I started at the Egon Shiele room, and in no time at all, I was stoned on beauty. They are gorgeous, erotic nudes from the turn of the nineteenth century. I climbed the stairs and stared at the paintings in the Klimt room, especially at Adele, so beautiful surrounded in gold and patterns.

In another room, I came upon an exhibit of old porno movies mounted on the wall. They were all rather decorous, involving buxom Victorian women disrobing and heading down to a small lake where they swam nude. I stared at the quaint, old-fashioned footage thinking about my boys and about the rawness, the crassness, and the lack of mystery in the sex they've been exposed to all their lives; everywhere they look, someone is fully exposed, if not XXX-rated. And that's just what's out in the open. God knows what they see alone in their rooms and the effect of that on their psyches, their sexuality, their views of men and women. All of this made me sad.

I was so lost in thought, I didn't notice that a man was standing next to me. Quite close, not exactly invading my personal space, but closer than is usual. He was a golden-skinned Indian man with jet black hair in a white shirt and khaki pants. His shoes were highly polished loafers with brass buckles. He turned to me and smiled. The whites of his eyes matched his sparkling teeth.

His accent was as beautiful as he was. Exactly like the imitation Jules always does of an East Indian.

"It must have been very risqué for its time."

I knew I was blushing because the man was absolutely gorgeous, and I wasn't used to gorgeous strangers talking to me. I lived in LA, after all, where casual encounters were not a part of my everyday life.

"It feels a little risqué now, to tell you the truth."

We both smiled.

I remember thinking what a switch from Healthy Harriet!

"Do you live in the city?"

"I wish. I live in LA now, though I used to live here. I'm in town for parents' day at my son's college."

"It is not possible for you to have a grown son."

"Really?" I said like an idiot. "I have two grown sons."

"Impossible!" my pick-up replied gravely.

The gallery that was empty when I arrived had now started to fill up with people. I moved on. And the handsome Indian man followed me.

We were now standing in front of yet another sexy nude. The Neue is a very hot spot. Though nothing like this had ever happened to me here before. We stood side by side, looking at her. One hand was over her breast, another at her crotch, her long reddish hair was loose over her bare shoulders and she had a look of languid happiness on her face.

I was nervous so I took a breath and smelled him next to me. A clean, spicy odor that made me think of curry, the *Kama Sutra*, sweet spiced chai, and lots of other pleasurable things as well.

He handed me a card. Our hands touched briefly and I thought of leading him down the marble stairs with the iron railings to the basement where the lavatories were. Or back to his lair, a hotel, an apartment, or even just a quiet place under the trees a few blocks away in Central Park. But of course, being Healthy Harriet, the minute I started undressing us, I then thought of herpes, HIV, and all sorts of other very unsexy stuff.

"If you have time, call me, we could go for a drink."

I took his card, smiled, and fantasized about calling Chandan Kumar the whole rest of the time I was in New York, but I never did. In fact, I still have his card.

Sam was great. I never had the slightest worries about Sam once he left home, or even when he was home, even with all the pot smoking, the sleeping late, the tattoo, the waxed, spiked hair, and horrible clothes he was always sunny Sam, wholesome and happy.

Gloria took us to dinner that first night.

Sam met me there. We were huddled in the corner of her huge living room. Gloria is fun to imitate and laugh about, but in person she's formidable. A real doyenne! Dan oddly is the only one of us who doesn't find her daunting and he calls her on the phone sometimes to just chat. He says she's a lonely old lady who needs understanding and everyone should be nicer to her.

"How's Columbia, Jules?" This she addressed to Sam.

"I'm Sam at NYU."

"Your brother doesn't wear his hair like you, sticking straight up like a porcupine."

Sam shrugged and squeezed my hand. It was

heaven, even in Gloria's awful living room, to be sitting on a slippery chintz ottoman having my hand squeezed by Sam.

Then it was my turn.

"Are you still interested in health food, Harriet?"

"More than ever!"

"I hope you don't feed Jules that way. I watched your show; I didn't see the point."

"Unfortunately, you're not alone, my ratings aren't very good."

"Then why do it? No one's really interested in health food. It's too much like a diet."

Wonderful Sam piped up.

"I'm interested in health food. I love vegetables. Harriet could make anyone love vegetables, hers are so delicious!"

Dear, dear Sam. I was remembering when he was small and the babysitter didn't show up, I had to take both of them on a business call with me. I told them beforehand, they had to act just perfectly. I depended on them.

Dan, of course, sat quietly throughout the meeting, exerting self-control as he always did. But bubbly Sam was known to speak his mind and it wasn't always complimentary.

My prospective client sat us down in her kitchen. It was one of those incredible home kitchens, three times as large as the one I had, and it was obvious this one had never been used. I was the latest one of the people who would bring precooked food in to reheat in the microwave.

She offered Dan and Sam juice. My boys, thanks to me, were juice snobs. Only fresh, squeezed juice would do for them. Dan declined and asked for water. Sam took a couple swallows of his Tropicana, smiled, and said, "This is the most delicious juice I've ever had. Thank you so much!"

That's Sam: always loyal. Always on my side.

Gloria wasn't interested in Sam's loyalty. Or anything else about him.

Not that she was that interested in me, either.

"I hope you're not still a vegetarian. I made a reservation at Gallagher's because I assumed Jules would be here. Tell me, does Jules ever call his father?"

"Bob died, Gloria," I reminded her.

"It was Bill who died," said my mother-in-law with conviction.

"Bill is Freeman's father, he's still alive."

"You look like you could use a nice steak, Harriet."

"I don't eat steak."

"What does Jules make of this? Why didn't he come?"

"He had to work, Grandma," said Sam.

"I don't understand why your mother lets

him work so hard." This she said addressing me.

"There's nothing I can do about it."

Gloria seemed to think about this for a moment or two.

"Harry was the same way. Absolutely impossible. And of course it killed him."

Harry was the husband after Jules' father.

"Harry's still alive as far as I know."

"And how is Freeman? Tell me does he have a girlfriend? Is there anyone at all in the picture? He never calls. Not that Jules calls . . ."

I had the vegetable plate at Gallagher's, which was absolutely delicious but coated with butter and salt and afterward gave me a belly-ache. Sam had the biggest steak I've ever seen, blood rare. He enjoyed himself enormously and still had room to insist on a rich dessert.

We sent Gloria home in a cab, but I wanted to walk for a bit. Before Sam and I separated at the Fifty-Ninth Street subway station, I tried to pump him about Dan.

"Has he said anything to you about enlisting?"

"Ma, Dan's not gonna do that. He just likes to torture you."

"Are you sure?"

"Funny thing is, I can just see him as some asshole in a uniform, marching around, saluting.

I felt wretched. Like throwing up. "Don't say

that! Promise me if he says anything to you, you'll tell me."

"I'm not gonna rat my brother out."

"You have to rat him out!"

"Ma!" said Sam. We hugged tightly before he ran down the stairs to catch the #1 train.

Eight

I could hear Marco barking cheerily as I stepped out of the taxi on Sunday evening. My house was lit up and Jules, whom I thought would be at work, was home and had company, someone who had arrived on a gleaming Harley Davidson. It was the kind Jules admired with the fancy saddlebags on the side.

It was the first time I'd been away from Marco and our reunion was yippy and heartfelt. Marco kept leaping up in the air expressing his delight to see me. I hadn't been so enthusiastically greeted since the boys were little.

Jules was in the kitchen by himself, surrounded by all sorts of stuff he'd pulled from the freezer. When I'm not around to make fresh, Jules has no trouble making do. He was having chili and brown rice, collard greens, corn bread, and some fresh fruit that I'd advised Valentina to prepare and put in a tight container so it would last a couple of days.

I had Marco in my arms, squirming his delight and licking my face. I went over to Jules and kissed him on top of his head.

"Hey, no lips that touched the dog's lips touching me, especially when I'm eating! I love Marco too, but I'm not as tribal as you are, Harriet."

I set Marco down.

"What's that Hells Angels thing doing in our driveway?"

"Oh," Jules said absently, as if it didn't matter. "It belongs to an editor I know whose on location in New York for a while. He's loaning it to me."

Then he changed the subject.

"How's Gloria? How's Sam?"

"Sam's wonderful. Gloria is Gloria; same as ever. Hey, did you see Lydia?"

"Yeah, the English chick. I've never seen Pasha take to anyone like that."

Just then, Jules' phone went off. The text tone . . . he looked down, smiled, and texted back.

"Who was that?"

"Someone from work."

"I was surprised to see you home at all."

"We wrapped early. Hey, put on a pair of jeans and we'll go for a spin down to the ocean. It's gorgeous."

"Jules, I'm sort of tired, I'm going to take a shower and play with Marco then take him for a walk."

"What's-her-name walked him. She took him to the mountains. He's had plenty of exercise."

"Maybe I feel too grown up to ride around on a motorcycle."

"You're the same age I am."

"But you're so immature."

Lydia and I met again a few days later. I had set it up with Jules that he would read her script. Then, if it was good (and I knew it would be) he'd call Freeman and we'd all get together and help Lydia with her career. Freeman's agency reps some of the biggest names around.

"That's Jules' brother?"

"Half-brother. Different fathers. That's why they have different last names."

Lydia sighed a huge sigh of sheer emotion.

"Harriet, you're brilliant!"

"I'll give you Jules' email. Just so you know, the deferential sweet young thing will work really well with him."

"Of course," said Lydia sagely, "he's a man."

"But it's a fine balance. He's very exacting. Don't lay it on too thick or he'll think you're playing him. He's quite paranoid. Also, he said to send it in a PDF file, so don't even think about sending it any other way."

We were at Mrs. Winston's. On the top-five list of what I will miss most about LA: the salads from there.

And not just any old salads; every day there is a new array of the freshest local organic fare California is known for. You make your own and go outside and sit under an umbrella. It's heaven!

We had Marco tied to a chair and were ooh-ing and aah-ing over our plates that were piled high. I noticed Lydia, like me, had picked water-cress, sprouts, avocado, squash, dark red basil, string beans. Our plates were almost identical, down to the choice of whole grain instead of white bread. She didn't have a kombucha, how-ever. She said they made her sick. I could drink kombucha—a bitter fermented tea that always makes me feel the Goddess is in her heaven after drinking one—morning, noon, and night.

Lydia reached over and took my hand.

"Thank you, Harriet. What can I do in return? Will you let me watch Marco again when you two go to visit Dan next weekend?"

"I accept. But Jules isn't coming."

"That's a shame."

"That's the way it is. I think sometimes it's my fault I can't get him to act like a dad unless he's in the mood. Though honestly, I wouldn't know what a dad was if one fell from the sky."

"That's also a shame. Having a father is wonderful. I'm a proud Daddy's girl!" Lydia's confident smile made me know this was no exaggeration.

"Lucky you!"

"My ex resented it."

"Is that what broke up the marriage?"

"We wanted different things, Harriet. Mostly I was tired of being a poor student. And I want a baby!"

"I remember! It's only lately I've had any money at all. I did catering up until my show."

"But you had Jules."

"I did and I didn't. I'm not exactly on the family-money gravy train, though the boys will be. He keeps it separate."

"Family money; how very lucky!"

"If you met his family, you wouldn't say lucky."

A homeless man approached our table then. Lydia firmly stood her ground and indicated to him, "No way."

I can never look the other way; I've been told I should avoid India, Mexico, or anyplace poor because I'd be torn to pieces.

I handed this guy a couple of ones and he headed off satisfied.

"Maybe Jules thinks you'll give away all his money."

"Funny you should say that. Jules always says I give everything away."

Valentina was furious that I didn't ask her to take Marco home.

The two of us were baking cookies with real sugar, organic turbinado, because I wanted to bring Dan real cookies so he wouldn't think I was still such a stick-in-the-mud.

I was creaming butter and sugar in one of the striped mixing bowls. Lately I'd been baking only olive-oil cookies and I was newly appreciating the alchemy that occurs when you pair sugar with butter. And the smell! Better than anything made with healthy olive oil. I stuck my pinky finger in and tasted a bit.

"Why you ask her and not me? Angel, he love dogs."

"She took care of him last time. By the way, how is Angel doing?"

"Angel not doing so good. The teacher called."

I put the bowl down, feeling guilty, guilty, guilty! I hated the idea of Angel, who I've known for years and is a smart boy, going to waste in the horrible schools in downtown LA.

"When I get back from Chicago we'll get on this. Don't forget."

"Harriet, I want Marco! Jesus will pick us up in the truck."

"I already asked her. It's too late."

And it was. I wish I had let Valentina take

him home. Maybe it would have happened anyway, but maybe I would have gotten to have
Marco just a little while longer.

That evening, as I was about to turn out the
light, I heard the now-familiar sound of the borrowed Harley motor pulling in the driveway.

Even before the front door opened, Marco
had jumped out of his basket, tail wagging at
ninety miles an hour, and was scooting merrily
down the stairs to greet Jules, whom he adored.
I thought they sort of looked alike.

"That's my good little boy," I heard Jules
cooing from downstairs. It was amazing how
bonded the two of them were.

I looked up. Jules, holding Marco, was now
in the doorway of our bedroom, all in black with
a brand-new jacket and boots. His hair was
sticking up from having been under the helmet.
He looked gorgeous and slick and nasty. And
yes, sexy as hell.

"Wow Jules, you look so wild!"

"Wild and groovy Jules. Maybe you need to
get some wild clothes too, woman. Go to Beverly Hills. Get yourself a motorcycle jacket and
boots and charge it to me. My treat!"

He put Marco down and dusted himself off.
Marco's little white hairs were everywhere, no
matter how often we vacuumed. Jules, in a rare
spirit of doing household chores, had come
home with a dozen of those rolls of adhesive

tape that are supposed to do the trick but never quite do. He was rolling his pants now with one of them.

"Just make sure you give that thing back before Thanksgiving. I don't want the boys thinking it's okay to have a motorcycle."

"I forgot to tell you," Jules replied laconically, "I bought it."

I should have known.

"There was no editor lending it to you. It was yours all along."

He set down the roll of adhesive. "In a manner of speaking."

I knew better than to argue with Jules. The motorcycle was a done deal, just like the movies that turned up two weeks before he had to leave for several months were a done deal. Jules had to own all the power and the right of scheduling. And especially the right of not consulting his wife on anything important to him.

"When are you coming back?" he asked, as though I was abandoning him.

"Sunday, you could come you know."

"Sam won't even notice."

"It's not Sam, that was last time. Sam's in New York and you were ducking your mother. This is Dan in Chicago."

"I could have sworn I wrote down Sam."

"I've never understood why you have so much trouble distinguishing between the two of them, they're quite different."

"You've gotten so hostile lately, Harriet."

For once I didn't take the bait.

"Lydia's taking care of Marco again. She'll come in and feed the cat if you want her to."

"That's okay; I'll take care of Pasha. I read her script, by the way."

"And?"

"Not bad. A bit pretentious. Too many stage directions, but that's to be expected. But better than I thought it would be."

High praise indeed, from critical Jules.

"Good, good, good! You'll call Freeman; we'll all go out to dinner."

Jules took off his jacket and hung it up lovingly on a big wooden hanger. Then he sat down at the foot of the bed and pulled off his boots. Then he slid off the special motorcycle pants.

After the boots, of course, he had to go wash his hands. He washed and he washed.

He called out over the running water.

"I don't know if I can face Freeman."

"He's not so bad."

Jules, who was just in his underwear now, looked like a giant baby with his slight pot belly, his skinny legs, and bandy knees. In those days I was in the habit of dressing Jules in strange costumes in my mind. When he acted like a baby, as he was then, I put him in a ruffled pinafore over his hairy chest and stuck a pacifier in his mouth. I wasn't imagining this because I thought he was a drag queen—no, far from that, he was a very hairy male who also happened to be a hysterical ninny and a huge baby.

"Freeman's not so bad, Jules," I said again.

Jules went to his dresser and pulled out a pair of sweat pants and some socks. Then a ski undershirt. He was always so cold. He claimed his coldness had to do with when he was little, Gloria being too cheap to ever buy him a decent coat. Poor little Oliver Twist Prince with Mrs. Jellyby as his mother.

"He's a fucking suit. He's been a suit all his life. And those teeth; they look like Chiclets. He told me he had to sell stock to pay for his inlays."

"Then I'll call him. I'll call your mother afterwards and tell her we're all going out to dinner. I wish she would learn to do email. I hate calling her on the phone—"

Nine

DAN DIDN'T EXACTLY STAND ME UP FOR DINNER THE night I arrived in Chicago. But it felt that way. I called him as soon as I got to the hotel and he said he didn't know what time he'd be done.

"Fine," I said, trying to sound like I didn't care. But when I hung up the phone, I cried a little. Then I washed my face, went out on the street, and found a fabulous sushi restaurant and ate sixty-five dollars worth of it with some really good sake that cost almost as much.

No strange, handsome men tried to pick me up in the sushi bar. I went back to my hotel and took a sleeping pill.

Dan refused to attend any events for parents' weekend. But Sam, who was far more conventional, had pulled the same thing. I didn't care. In a way, I was secretly relieved not to be sitting husbandless and fatherless with all the normal couples, the way it had always been at school events because Jules never showed up.

I was here to visit with Dan, I told myself, and to get just a peek at his life if he'd let me. He finally arrived at my hotel to pick me up late the next afternoon. By then I'd been to the Art Institute and for another fancy meal, though it didn't cheer me up like dinner had the night before. And again, no one paid me any attention anywhere.

He had a borrowed car and we drove to the South Side of Chicago where the campus was. He took me back to his room, a private one he had negotiated all on his own that was so small two people standing up in it felt a little like the subway car at rush hour. Dan always negotiated everything all on his own: college entrance forms, essays, he only took me to the tours because you can't rent a car at seventeen. His room was neat, but I'd been expecting that.

"I've got something to tell you," he said almost right away.

I nodded, sat down on his narrow bed, and imagined a scene from a war movie. Probably a very outdated war movie. I try and avoid war movies whenever possible. I was seeing men in camouflage, bombs going off, shrieks of agony. The American flag falling down and some bloodied arm hoisting it up.

"You don't have to look so scared. It's a good thing, Harriet."

"Yeah?"

"Yeah! I'm in therapy here. I'm not going to any lousy school shrink; I called up Gloria and she's funneling some of my trust money. She was very understanding. I don't know why you don't like her. She likes you."

"You could have fooled me," I replied. "But go on, tell me about the therapy."

"I interviewed a bunch of shrinks. The one I picked isn't on Jules' health plan. Your insurance doesn't cover shrinks. Did you know that?"

"Yes," I replied.

"You should go," he said, "hit up the old man for the money. That's why I hit up Gloria. It's very expensive."

"I know," I said. "And you're probably right, I should go."

"He's much better than the guy you sent me to back home."

Obviously shrink picking is not my forte. So why bother?

I nodded my head, trying to look encouraging.

"That stuff with the lifeboat growing up. That was really fucked up. I've got the old man's voice inside me saying, "You're doing it wrong, you're doing it wrong! You're not good enough for the lifeboat. I'm okay the way I am."

"Of course you are, Dan!"

"It didn't help, you always overcompensating, being the nice one, sneaking us money. Maybe you let him do all the dirty work. Maybe you're afraid of your own hostility. Maybe Dad is your dark side! Have you ever read Jung?"

I looked at Dan, totally shocked. Because I had in fact gone through a phase of reading Jung. Maybe he was right and Jules was my shadow.

"Thank you for telling me that," I said, and I meant it. "Is there anything else you'd like to tell me?"

Just then, there came a knocking at the door. Dan went for it. Presently, he introduced me to Indira, a beautiful East Indian girl who looked eons older than Dan. And was. She was already in graduate school. How come all these sexy East Indians were turning up? Was it my love affair with yoga, or just coincidence?

"I'm very pleased to meet you, Mrs. Prince."

"Harriet please!"

"Dan and I have watched your show. I enjoy it very much."

"Really?" I asked like a total idiot. "You watched my show?"

Dan, who had his arm around Indira, said, "Indira sprouts mung beans at her apartment just like you do at home. Her mung is spicier than yours. But it's still mung!"

I had no idea I had made any impression on Dan at all in recent years except one of disappointment, and, worse than that, contempt. And here he was touting my mung. I was proud and elated. And full of hope for the future of our relationship.

"Let's go somewhere really special," I gushed. "In fact, let's go eat some mung beans."

We enjoyed a wonderful evening, Dan, Indira, and I. Indira is studying for her masters in political science and had gotten Dan interested in the subject. No word was mentioned about enlisting.

I hadn't felt so happy in ages.

I called Jules when I got back to the hotel to tell him about Indira, but he didn't pick up. I texted him about Indira but he didn't text back. Clearly, he was telling the truth this time and must be up to his neck in reshoots.

Ten

I ARRIVED HOME EARLY IN THE EVENING ON SUNDAY. Jules' Beemer that he hardly used anymore was in the driveway with its chock up against the back wheel. He was on the Harley, obviously. Lydia's bright blue Mazda with the *Write Like A Girl* sticker on the back bumper was parked in front.

I opened our front door and heard Marco's happy yip. Soon he had jumped into my arms and I headed with him back to the kitchen.

Lydia was sitting at the table with Pasha in her lap, stroking his head. It was a comforting sight, my new friend with Pasha in her lap, sitting in my kitchen.

I put Marco down. He went for his little basket and plopped there.

"I just got in from the mountains," she said. "We had a marvelous time. But I wanted Pasha to know he's in my heart too." Lovely Lydia continued to stroke Pasha, whose purring filled the kitchen.

"Thank you so much! Let's have a drink or a cup of tea. Which will it be?"

"Tea please," Lydia replied, "I've got greeting cards to write this evening, not that I need sobriety to do that, but it will go faster."

Pasha jumped down from her lap and went over to where Marco was in his little basket. The two of them curled into each other companionably for once.

"So how was Dan?"

I began to tell her about the weekend, about Indira. How relieved I was that my son seemed happy and wasn't muttering a word about enlisting.

Before I could tell her about Freeman and how we were all going out to dinner, I heard the sound of Jules' motorcycle outside.

"That's my Hells Angel!" I said idiotically.

I went to the back door and stepped outside, thinking I would greet him.

Some things in life change gradually, so gradually you aren't aware of the change even happening. But not then, not that night. Tragedy arrived like a sudden cold snap, leaving us shivering and shocked. I stepped out the back door, and Pasha was right behind me, Marco behind him. Then in a sudden flash of fur chasing fur, the two of them were out the back door along the side of the house. Pasha, being a cat, used up one of his nine lives. But Marco ran right into Jules' brand-new Harley that was turning in the driveway.

According to Jules, it knocked Marco way up in the air in an arc. Jules thought it was all going to be okay, that maybe he would only break a bone because there wasn't all that much blood and he was still moving when he hit the ground.

By the time I got there, he was just trembling. Heartbreaking little whimpers. More trembling. And his adorable little tail kept wagging all the time. I didn't want to move him. But I was right next to him, trying to comfort him. Then, all at once, a shudder wracked his little body and another terrible tremble. Then no trembling at all. His tail stopped. Pasha slunk back into the house, his mission accomplished.

I continued to sit there with my dead puppy, stroking his little head.

"Are you sure he's dead?" Jules shouted.

"Yes," I replied. I knew some CPR and had taken every Red Cross course there was when the boys were small. I checked for his vital signs and there weren't any. My dog was so terribly still it couldn't mean anything but dead. I put my hand at his heart again, remembering its warm, hearty pump. Nothing now.

"There wasn't anything I could do," Jules

whimpered. I had never seen him even close to tears. Not even at his father's funeral.

"They both were running. Pasha chasing Marco. He ran right in front of my bike."

"If it was anybody's fault, it was mine," I said quietly. "I'm the one who left the back door open."

Jules didn't admonish me, thank God. There are limits. Even Jules knows that, when push comes to shove.

Then Lydia was beside us. She got down on the ground with me and Marco. She put both her long arms around me. She was crying, unlike me. I was too stunned to cry.

"He had a beautiful time with you. And a quick end. It's more than most of us get, Harriet."

Jules and Lydia went in the house. I refused to move. They came back with one of my prettiest blankets from the linen closet. This we wrapped Marco in; he was already turning cold. Then we all went inside. I laid Marco in the laundry room and shut the door.

Lydia took over, she was now in command. She put the kettle on and served me a strong cup with sugar in it the way you're supposed to if someone has had a shock.

Jules went upstairs. When he came back down his motorcycle clothes were off and he was in his normal jeans and a pressed shirt.

"I've found someone to pick up Marco. She'll be here soon."

We sat around the kitchen table, Lydia, Jules, and I. Pasha had taken over Marco's little basket and was purring away like the evil predator he was.

The woman who picked up Marco was middle aged, dumpy, and had a small precise, mustache. She was very business-like and kind. She asked me if I wanted the ashes.

"Not really," I answered. What was I going to do? Scatter Marco's remains over the sidewalks in my neighborhood? They don't allow dogs at the beach near where we live. It wasn't as if I'd be taking him back to one of his favorite places. Everyplace was his favorite place! He had been the happiest, most agreeable dog imaginable.

But I did end up creating a crash shrine in front of the house. I took stones from the back yard and I bought some candles, the kind with the Saints on them and three with the Virgin Mary (who has always seemed to me a lot hipper than the Saints, except of course St. Francis). I bought a bunch of them, but they wouldn't all stay lit.

Jules, being Jules, claimed they were a fire hazard, and perhaps they were.

"How long are you going to keep that thing going outside? It makes me feel like shit and it looks so cheesy."

It was a few days later. I was at the sink rinsing beans, back to cooking.

"What did you say?"

"Is that picture of Jesus autographed?"

"Valentina gave me that picture. I never told you this, but she had a premonition. She did everything she could to take Marco home with her that weekend."

"Valentina and her premonitions. I wish she'd have a word from above to wash her hands."

"God dammit, Jules, stop being so fucking flip. Our dog died there, under the wheels of your midlife crisis."

"I thought we agreed not to blame each other, Harriet."

"We did and I'm sorry." Then I started sobbing again. I dried my tears with a dish towel.

"The boys didn't even get to meet Marco."

"It gives me the willies having that thing in front."

"It's supposed to give you the willies, it's a crash shrine."

Jules left the room. I made some soup with all the leftover vegetables we had in the fridge. It was market day tomorrow. And if I had vegetables left over that's what I always did, made soup with them. Looking back, I really was a balabusta like Jules always said. I wonder if he ever misses me.

Eleven

THAT AFTERNOON, I HAD TOLD LYDIA SHE SHOULD MOVE in with us since she didn't yet have a place to live. I'd even called up Dan and gotten the okay for her to use his room temporarily. Sam was coming home for Thanksgiving, but not Dan. Dan and Indira were going to have Thanksgiving dinner with all their friends.

All that week, Jules came home at reasonable times. We talked about how weird it was without little Marco, who had, in such a short time, become such an important part of us. We were both kind to one another, never pointing a finger or saying it was your fault. I remember he was watching AMC, some old black-and-white movie with lots of shadows, when I sat down next to him on the couch and told him about Lydia moving in.

Since I've spent months and months trying to understand exactly what went down at our house during that crucial period of time, I remember distinctly Jules not taking to the idea of it so well. Was it already an idea in his mind? Was it already something of a done deal in reality? Valentina had somehow "seen" the death of Marco. Right away she had treated Lydia like an enemy. But I wasn't thinking anything like that then. It was all still buried in the workings of my tortured subconscious. And of course I was in deep mourning for my puppy.

"What are you doing that for? You hate houseguests. When my mother stays here you're a basket case for weeks!"

"At least I deal with her. You just stay at work. Besides, Lydia's my friend. She doesn't have a place to live. And don't forget, we're having dinner with Freeman in exactly four days. Don't even think about trying to wiggle out of it."

"Where's she gonna stay?"

"Dan's room."

"Dan's not gonna like that."

"I've already gotten his okay."

"What, is he never coming home again?"

"He says he's planning to come home for Christmas."

"What about the English chick? What will she do when Dan comes home?"

"It's just temporary, Jules."

It was a casual evening at home with the two

of us. One of the last, now that I think of it. While Jules was watching a noir film that evening, I was fixing up Dan's room with the new stuff I'd bought that afternoon. A pretty, new comforter, sheets to match, I'd even bought some fancy hangers made out of satin and replaced the plastic ones in the neat and nearly empty closet Dan had left behind. I would put the girlie stuff away when he came home and only use it for company.

I remember Jules standing in the doorway.

"What's going on here? What are you doing to Dan's room? You really are serious about her moving in here, aren't you?" I remember he said, "her" and not "Lydia," like the important thing was houseguests in general, not her in particular. Maybe on some level this was reassuring. Maybe it gave me the illusion of control.

"It's just temporary; she needs a place to stay. Sam's room has so much junk in it, no one could stay there but Sam."

"Will she eat with us?"

"I don't know, I haven't thought about it. I suppose so, if she wants. I'm baking scones tomorrow for my show. I'm calling it 'Company's Coming.' I guess, on some level, I am thinking about it."

But I wasn't. At least I don't think I was. I was acting under my own radar.

If Jules was upset, Valentina really hit the roof.

"Now I know why you do that to Dan's room!"

"Yes," I said, feeling guilty. I don't know why I was feeling guilty, but Valentina has a way of provoking that in me. I wonder if she knows that.

"She needs a place to stay."

Valentina had her hands on her hips, her eyes were flashing, her dense dark hair trembling.

"Tell her no."

"I invited her."

"Marco just die, Harriet. He was like a baby to you. You need a new dog not a girl."

"I like her."

"She too pretty and young."

"You're pretty and young. Jules' mother is always warning me about you."

"I have Jesus and Angel. And Jules don't like me touching his things."

That made us both burst into laughter. We laughed and we laughed at Jules not letting her touch his things. It was the first time since little Marco died I felt even remotely human.

When we settled down, we sat at the old oak table in the kitchen as we often did and had a snack. We talked about Angel for a while. He was doing fine in math, in fact near the top of his class. It was English that bedeviled him. Valentina's written English is sort of scary. Every once in a while I'd get on her about going back to school, but I could never prevail.

"Lydia does tutoring, Valentina. I'll ask her. She'll tell us what to do."

Twelve

LYDIA MOVED IN THE NEXT AFTERNOON. LOOKING BACK on it, I appear absurdly cavalier about the whole thing. How could I have been so unaware that I was cooking something up? Or that my replacement, at my own request, was inside my house and there to stay? But what else could I have been thinking, moving this gorgeous creature in, who by her own admission wanted a baby and everything else that went with it? A self-avowed Daddy's girl (and we all know they want to take Daddy away from Mommy), one who I even helped schlep her four suitcases up to Dan's room. Just as I had helped Dan schlep his down to the taxicab when he left for college a couple of months before. The rest of Lydia's stuff, I was told, was in storage in downtown Los Angeles.

I wasn't thinking then, how could I have been, that I too would soon have a storage unit not too far from the cottage cheese plate. That I would be falling into my nightly Ambien stupor with the sound of the 405 freeway as my lullaby. And she would be the mistress of my house, not Jules' ripe young mistress, as she undoubtedly was by now.

I took her up to her room and she looked around as if she was bewildered.

"You've gone to quite a lot of trouble haven't you?" she said, like she wished I hadn't. She touched one of the seven vanilla bottles, each of which had a Gerber daisy. There was a white one on the chest of drawers, two pinks on the desk, and two reds and two yellows on the bedside table. I remember thinking the bright colors looked so pretty with the lavender quilt on the bed; how fun it was to have another female in the house after years and years of the all-boys show. And that seven was a lucky number. But lucky for whom? Lydia or me? Or was it just Jules as usual who was on the receiving end of all the female bounty?

Yes, those Gerbers were my last little touch, like the sugar flower on an elaborate butter cream cake of the kind I was not in the habit of baking and icing. Was she feeling guilty? By now she had gotten more than a taste of Jules, who, let me be the first to say, can be addictively delicious. Did she already plan to sink those white, shiny, un-Englishy teeth into him permanently? Was I cooperating with her plans or was she cooperating with mine?

That's the thing; I think whatever we did or didn't know about what was going to happen, we both knew that this was between the two of us. We were the bread on either side, and Jules was the filling sandwiched in between our desires. That both of us thought the other was unconscious made the situation far more potent.

I can see beautiful Lydia so clearly: her dark shiny hair, the whites of her eyes, the white of her teeth, and the black-and-white striped dress with those big boobs on top and the very long legs in tights on the bottom.

She was loading a suitcase onto the luggage rack when she turned to me.

"Still time to change your mind, Harriet."

"Why would I do that?"

"Houseguests can be a bore," she told me lightly.

"But you're not a guest; you're my friend, aren't you?"

And friends don't fuck other friend's husbands. But I didn't say that, or think that, or imply that in any way. But isn't that the unspoken agreement?

But I can see now, she was having feelings; why else would she say, gesturing to the redone room: "You must promise not to spoil me anymore."

"Okay, I promise."

By now Lydia was at the window that faced the street looking out. "I see you still have the shrine going. I hope you're feeling a little better at the moment."

"I am a little. I'm trying to anyway. I know one thing, I'll never forget him."

"Nor will I. Are you thinking about getting another? While I'm here, I'll help you."

"No."

Just then Pasha appeared in the doorway, gorgeous Pasha with his long stripes, his wide, beautiful head. He sprung up and settled himself squarely on Lydia's bed on the brand-new lavender quilt.

Lydia sat on the edge of the bed stroking my faithless Pasha.

"I'm afraid Pasha's quite happy to be the only four-footed creature in the house. Being an only child, I can sympathize."

"What's it like being an only child?"

Lydia considered this for a moment.

"Lonely actually, but you get used to it. There are other compensations."

"Like what?"

"Well, I've always known I was the center of the universe. And I get my way most of the time. And of course," she said patting the lavender quilt, "my own room."

It was easy to see the beautiful, confident woman sitting on my son's bed, stroking my cat, was a wanted child. My sons were wanted too. Even Jules, whose mother didn't give him nearly enough hugs, had somehow conveyed to him a sense of entitlement. Not me. My mother hadn't planned to have me. I came directly on the heels of my brother who was very much wanted. That's practically the first thing I ever learned about myself: I wasn't expected or wished for; I was a mistake.

What would it be like to know you're wanted, really, really wanted? I had no idea. I know how to make other people feel wanted, but have always felt uncomfortable if I wanted "things" myself. Perhaps this was the deep, silent core of me. One that would never change—and certainly not in the marriage with Jules, who not only felt perfectly comfortable not sharing what he had with me, but did his best to control me with money, with guilt, with superior verbal skills, whatever it took.

I remember walking over and giving Lydia a hug. In fact, I think that was the last hug I ever gave her.

"I hope you won't be lonely here. When you're done unpacking, you can put your suitcases in the garage. Are you hungry?"

"Starving!"

"Good, I waited lunch for you."

I turned and headed for the door. Lydia turned and started unpacking her stuff.

"Lydia!" I called out.

My beautiful friend whirled around to face me.

"Catch!" I called out and tossed her a set of keys, top lock and bottom. Lydia held up her hand, the keys grazed it, then clattered noisily to the floor.

Lydia took to bringing her laptop down to work at the kitchen table while I was cooking, late in the afternoon after Valentina left for the day.

"I feel so at home here!" she said more than once. "And I still can't get over that you have one of my favorite American poems tacked up on the board."

"I found that in an old cookbook a few weeks ago. It looks like I typed it. Do you believe I remember when people typed on typewriters!"

"Prelapsarian!"

"What does that mean?"

"Before the fall of man, in the heyday of the Garden of Eden."

"Ah," I said. "You have such a wonderful vocabulary!"

"Shall I recite it to you, Harriet?"

I turned around from my stirring and looked at her. Pasha, as usual, was curled on her lap. And she was stroking him when she wasn't tapping at her keyboard.

"I have eaten / the plums / that were in / the icebox // and which / you were probably / saving / for breakfast // Forgive me / they were delicious . . ."

Here she paused.

And I finished for her "so sweet / and so cold."

We continued to stare into each other's eyes for a moment. Instead of there being a closeness from the poem we both loved, it felt like a chill was now upon us. And I was scared suddenly. She was looking at me so coldly; it felt like she hated me. Or maybe I hated her. One of us was having strong feelings—or maybe both of us were. The air was so thick you could cut it with a knife.

I turned from her icy stare and walked over to the sink and rinsed some potatoes with the sprayer, it's a very hi-tech sprayer that packs a wallop. I remember distinctly having a sudden urge to turn around and aim the strong stream of water straight into Lydia's face, ruining her makeup, ruining her silky hairdo, maybe even dislodging the cute little thing she had keeping a lock of hair from falling in her eyes. Shocked a little at my own imagining, I put the sprayer down.

"When I was younger, I used to write poetry," I told my friend.

"I did too," Lydia admitted.

"Funny how something that's very important to you at one time ends up making so little difference in your life, until you read a few lines and there's this shocking sense of loss."

Lydia's face was different now, softer, like the face I knew and had invited into my house. She didn't hate me anymore, and I didn't hate her either. Exit the phantom sprayer.

"That's such a sad thing to say, Harriet, but it's beautiful too."

Tears were rolling down Lydia's cheeks. I remembered it was Lydia, and Lydia only, who had cried for Marco. Lydia had access to her tears. To her emotions. Not like me; I was too shut down most of the time to do anything but scream in sheer frustration.

But of course only someone seriously shut down could have been devising, however deviously, such a crushing coup d'état in her own home. A crushing coup d'état she had no idea was about to happen.

"I'm going to the seven thirty class. Do you want to come with me?"

"Only if it's slacker yoga. I can't face anything taxing at the moment."

"You better not then, the first time I took it, I could barely walk home."

We had the radio on and were listening to *Which Way LA?* so I didn't hear Jules' chock in the driveway. He hadn't taken the motorcycle to work. I was hoping he was getting sick of it. I was really hoping he'd even get rid of it like I asked him to before Sam came home for Thanksgiving. The door opened; there stood Jules in his normal work clothes carrying his normal leather man bag.

I gave him a brief kiss and told him I was off.

"Hey, where are you going, Harriet? What's for dinner?"

"Dinner's on the stove. Maybe you can talk Lydia into keeping you company."

That's, as far as I know, the only time they were alone together in the house when I was the boss of the kitchen.

When I got home from yoga, the dishwasher was running and the food was put away. Jules was watching the black-and-white movie channel and Lydia was up in her room doing whatever it was she did behind closed doors.

Yes, in a way we were the perfect family.

Thirteen

A FEW DAYS LATER, I CAME IN THE DOOR WITH THE fixings for dinner just as Lydia was leaving all dolled up, wearing a dress and war paint (discreet and tasteful war paint). Pasha was standing on one of the front hall steps meowing.

"Are you going to be here for dinner?"

"No, I'm meeting someone."

"Someone wonderful I hope."

"Well, we'll see. Perhaps he'll be fit for the lifeboat!"

Ah, the lifeboat. She was speaking in Jules' vernacular already. I didn't ask her how she knew about the lifeboat. I don't believe I had ever told her.

"Dan says the lifeboat wasn't good. He felt he never measured up."

"I can see how that could come to pass. Still, I told Jules I'm going to steal it for my next project."

When I said, "Jules certainly knows how to hit the nail on the head, doesn't he?" was I pimping her?"

"He's clever and funny and edgy. Yet civilized. One feels safe with him."

"Oh, he's been known to blow his top on occasion."

She replied with a smile and, "Ah, but he's on his good behavior with me." Was she pimping me?

I believe Lydia turned away just then.

"Harriet, after we talked I spoke to Valentina about Angel and I'm going to help him with his English."

"That's wonderful! You'll meet him at Thanksgiving next week. I really, really appreciate this Lydia."

"It's the least I can do."

After she left, I texted Jules who texted back that he was eating on the set but wouldn't be hugely late. And he was as good as his word, home by nine o'clock. Except that he hadn't eaten on the set and I gave him a plate of food.

"Where's Lydia?" he asked as soon as he walked in.

"Out on a date. She was all dressed up."

I wonder if the two of them met that night somewhere away from home and he was covering his tracks asking her whereabouts.

Later on that same evening, Jules and I were

watching *Rebecca* on TV when Lydia came in, put her purse down, and sat on the couch next to me.

Now it was the three of us watching the movie, transfixed. Pasha was curled up on Lydia's lap.

I can still see Olivier telling Joan Fontaine, "I never loved Rebecca, I hated her!" I had seen it half a dozen times but it always thrilled me.

After it was over, the three of us went into the kitchen for a snack. Jules, being Jules, had cereal before bed like all children do.

Lydia was having a glass of white wine and some cashew nuts.

I had a thimble of Amontillado, some filberts, and a small Pink Lady that was crisp and sweet.

"So how was your date, Lydia?" This from Jules.

"Quite nice, actually. I'm thinking he's lifeboat material."

Jules laughed. "Indeed?"

"Indeed!"

They smiled at each other then. In fact, they looked terribly happy to be looking at one another. Furthermore, I think from then on, every time I looked up they seemed to be lost in each other's eyes and smiles.

Probably they were speaking in code, and probably on some level I knew it. I got up, rinsed my dish, and yawned elaborately.

"I'm up past my bedtime." And I was. It was eleven already and though I didn't have to get up the next day, I needed sleep for later in the week when I would be. "I'm going to bed. Night, night!" I called out.

Then I left the kitchen, turned into the hallway, and sat down on the dark stairs; out of sight but not out of hearing.

"*Rebecca*'s one of my favorites." This from Lydia. "It's so clever how they never actually name the new wife. In the novel du Maurier never mentions her name either."

Jules sounded very cute, "I'm a *Shadow of Doubt* Man. It was Hitchcock's favorite movie."

"Really? I wasn't aware."

"Don't they teach you anything at film school?"

"Apparently not, Jules!"

No, nothing suggestive passed between them, but Jules is very paranoid and would never do such a dangerous thing in his own house. However, I'm fairly sure it was starting to occur to me that these two were getting very close and there was something in the air. Why else would I have been spying on them?

I'm quite sure Freeman's competing with Jules for Lydia clinched the deal. The New Me, in a way, was fueled by this biblical drama. When you have a cold, indifferent mother like Gloria, it's only natural that you would feel deprived and believe the other brother got more than you.

That "Freeman" is more of a name than "Jules" certainly never made the grown up situation any rosier. Jules may call his half brother a suit; he may laugh at his expensive dental work and his fancy shoes; he can snicker over his silk pocket squares and his Porsche that has an automatic transmission, but the fact remains, Freeman makes far more money as an A-list talent agent than Jules does as a B-list working cameraman. And Jules hates him for it. Perhaps that's why he couldn't help but deny our boys his unconditional love, because he knew they came first with me.

We were waiting for Freeman a few evenings later. We were at the kind of restaurant Jules hates most: fusion (which, according to Jules, means combining nothing with nothing), Beverly Hills, air-kissing, super expensive, and populated by the most conspicuous members of the in-crowd. Worse than all this, the waiter wasn't paying any attention to us. We weren't "in" enough for that. I could feel Jules' foot tapping crazily under the table, a sure sign that he's about to lose it. And he was very close to losing it, to having his 'strawberry moment.'

So far, Jules had been charm itself in front of

our houseguest. No temper tantrums, no ranting and raving about Valentina's lack of cleanliness, moron directors, hostile PC assholes who drive Priuses, or national news. His own obsessive hand cleaning was under wraps too. Our usual three rolls of paper towels a day was down to two since her arrival.

Still and all, I knew the fusion joint in Beverly Hills was a perfect opportunity for a Jules-style shit fit. And some of me was aware that if it happened, Lydia wouldn't look at him with such shining eyes. Yes, even then I was conflicted; part of me wanted him to show his true colors. Part of me wanted him to look good in front of Lydia. I was at war with myself and my desires. And still dangerously in denial about the true state of our little triangular nation.

Jules kept fiddling with the salt and pepper shakers. Knocking them together. Rearranging them. And his foot kept dancing underneath the table.

If she sees him like that, she'll run away, I thought. We'll both run away, we'll have a mutiny!

Jules' voice was just on the edge of really nasty.

"The service here sucks. Freeman's late, he might even be standing us up."

When I spied Freeman seconds later, I was momentarily disappointed; I sort of wanted

Jules to show his true colors.

I waved.

Freeman was heading our way, but not losing the opportunity to work the room. Yes, it seemed everybody in the whole place was on a kissing level with Freeman, who arrived at our table with several different shades of lipstick on his cheeks. Real kisses, not air kisses, apparently.

Jules' contemptuous muttering was now under control.

"He'll be working the room at his own funeral. He'll rise from the coffin . . ."

Jules didn't have a chance to finish his sarcasm because Freeman was now at the table with us. I'd forgotten how much taller he is than Jules, who, although not small, is fine boned. Freeman is wide shouldered, and now in middle age, wolfish with a paunch.

The two men exchanged a half-hearted Hollywood hug. I tried to infuse more warmth into my greeting. I sort of like Freeman.

"And you're Lydia who went to Cambridge and film school. I went to business school in London."

"LSE?" Lydia wanted to know, and for a moment I hated her.

Jules piped up, "Now, now, Freeman, tell Lydia the truth, you only lasted one semester in London. You've got lipstick on your face, by the way."

"That Julia wears too much lipstick," he smiled, then mopped at his face with a napkin. A waiter was now at our table bowing and scraping and fawning.

"Good evening, sir. It's my pleasure to serve you, sir."

"I'll have the Maker's Manhattan straight up. Lydia will you join me?"

"Absolutely."

Jules asked for bubbly water and I opted for a merlot.

Freeman's phone went off. "Excuse me, I've got to take this call," then dropped another first name.

Jules looked disgusted, but now insisted he had to make a call too. Presently he was saying, "Have you had a chance to look at the dalies?"

I turned to Lydia. "Shall we call each other or do you want to have your girl call my girl?"

Lydia laughed. "They can't have babies, Harriet. They have to do something to while away their time." And when she said this, I fell in love with her all over again.

The food really was out of this world. I had something with millet, pine nuts, and Morrel mushrooms with just a hint of sherry. The tea afterward, an Assam, was stunning with wild honey instead of white sugar. Jules ate every morsel of his huge pork chop. Lydia, the same with her lamb chop. Freeman had a course with sea urchin served on a veritable coral reef and a lobster salad with the meat served in the shell; the two most expensive items on the menu. But he made a huge show of picking up the check and with his wolfish grin turned to Lydia.

"Nothing I like better than mixing business with pleasure." Jules kicked me under the table just in case I missed how corny the line was.

Freeman took Lydia's arm on the way out, and stopped to introduce her to a couple of other famous first names. Lydia was flushed from the Maker's Manhattans and perhaps from proximity to so many famous names. But she remained cool and I had to admire her for not letting all this luminary shit go to her head.

As we were standing by the door, waiting for the cars, Freeman said to Lydia, "So we're all set. You'll shoot me the script. I'll read it and we'll go from there."

"Marvelous!"

I asked Freeman whether he wanted to come to Thanksgiving and when he said he might be going to Paris but wouldn't know for a few days, we left it open.

"You can just show up," I assured him. "Bring someone if you like."

PART III

Fourteen

THE LAST THANKSGIVING AT MY HOUSE WAS ONE OF MY best, I think. Sam, who adores stuffing—my stuffing in particular—said I outdid myself. Food, I have noticed, often comes out better when there's a certain amount of emotional intensity going on. The flavors meld better; the crisp food is crisper, the tangy is tangier, and so forth. And ah the sweet parts! Did the fact that at least three of us knew, on some level, a showdown was coming, make the pleasure of this feast sharper as well as sweeter?

Have I mentioned Thanksgiving is my very favorite holiday? The only one I feel even slightly sentimental about. Jules is right; I'm the only Jew anyone knows who hates Christmas. Chanukah, though I tried to promote it around our house, is always such a lackluster second, no matter what you do. No one is ever dreaming of a white Chanukah—and of course a Jew wrote that song about Christmas.

I have always made a big deal out of Thanksgiving, trying to keep it healthy within reason, of course. I don't do that thing where you have mashed potatoes, creamed onions, stuffing, yams, cornbread, and dessert. No, years ago I gave up on the mashed potatoes and the creamed onions, and I never put yucky marshmallow or sweet stuff on my yams. But I make all the rest starting three days before with the homemade cranberry chutney my friend Susan (another expat Southerner) invented.

That Thanksgiving morning was the last time Jules ever reached for me.

Naturally he knew I had to get up and take the turkey out of the fridge. You can't leave a turkey out, even unstuffed, overnight. He's also been with me for so many Thanksgiving feasts, he knows what a nervous wreck I am every single year.

He went for me, in the dark, the second the alarm went off.

"Happy Thanksgiving!" he whispered, kissing my neck and wrapping one of his warm, hairy legs around mine.

"You need to shave your legs, Harriet, you feel like you've got barbed wire growing on them. In fact, you could rent them out to an empty lot in the South Bronx."

I squirmed away.

"Ah, come on, Harriet, I was trying to make you laugh. Where's our holiday cheer?"

"I've got thirteen people coming at three o'clock and I'd like to take a run before I start everything."

"Getting off is good for you!" said Dr. Jules. And I knew he was right. We hadn't done it in a good while. At least a month. I lay back and tried to get into it, when he bit one of my breasts just a bit too hard. He knows I hate that.

"Ouch!" I told him, "that really hurts." Then I sat up in bed.

And Jules replied, "Go take your fucking run."

My running clothes were all laid out. I hastily got into them then headed downstairs and out the door.

Dan called at 8:00 a.m. It was already ten in Chicago.

"You're basting! That's fabulous."

All at once the tears that didn't fall when Marco died came cascading down my cheeks at the thought of Dan being all grown up, with his very grown up girlfriend, earnestly cooking his very first turkey. What a rite of passage. Like the driver's test. Or losing one's virginity. A couple of weeks ago, I had sent a long email about the process of making stuffing: The drying of the bread, the sautéing of the vegetables, how you sweat them, not brown them. And I shared with him something I only started instigating a couple of years ago that saves enormous amounts of time. Buy French bottled chestnuts (not Chinese that come in a packet) for eight zillion bucks instead of fresh with all the scoring, roasting and pealing. And moisten the dried out bread all at once with stock, wine, and sherry—Marsala, if it's around—instead of dipping each individual piece in the liquid like Noog, my mother's housekeeper, had taught me to do all those years ago. I'd put some extra money in Dan's checking account so he could buy the best organic turkey and splurge on the chestnuts that are eight times as expensive.

I was telling him now about basting. "Use whatever old wine you have in the house. You can use orange juice, bourbon, whatever, just keep the bird moist."

I, who had decided this year that I wouldn't even make an exception and have turkey on Thanksgiving, had so many elaborate theories about how to make the dead bird more tasty. Now, I don't give a flying fuck; meat, to me, is awful and I won't even touch it for folding green.

"You'll know it's done when you wiggle the leg a little and poke it with a fork. If the juices are clear, you're done."

He and Indira were having at least ten people over. I was so excited for them.

Dan even told me he loved me. The best Thanksgiving present I could get. Dan hadn't told me he loved me in years.

After I hung up I ran around the kitchen thinking about Marco, being immeasurably sad he wouldn't be here for his first plate of Thanksgiving turkey. I was regretting, too, that I hadn't had sex with Jules. Why was I being so withholding? Especially when I was actually pretty horny.

I was thinking about all the Thanksgivings we'd done together. How Jules' father had been at a few. And Gloria too with one of her later husbands. Family! Other than our boys, Jules and I didn't really have family. I wondered if Freeman was going to show up. My guess was that he would.

Thank God Sam was coming home.

Jules appeared presently, shiny from his shower, holding the newspaper. Then Lydia, also fresh as a flower. Both of them sat down at the table.

"This is Harriet's idea of a good time," Jules remarked. "You've got flour on your face."

"Make yourself a coffee," I said to Lydia, gesturing to the ersatz espresso machine we all love. "And look over there on the counter, pumpkin spelt muffins for breakfast. No sugar and all whole grain; there will be plenty of bad stuff later on."

Jules smirked. "Just once we should all go to a restaurant and get waited on."

"You'd hate it!" I assured him.

"And what would you do with so much free time?"

Yes, we were sparring with each other a bit in front of Lydia. But she appeared unfazed.

"I'd like to help," she said.

"Valentina, Angel, and Jesus will be here soon. You'll get to meet Angel."

"We've been in contact; he's going to bring the assignment for the book he's supposed to write about. Everything's under control."

Jules announced, "I texted Sam last night just to bring a backpack. That way I can pick him up on the bike. We can bypass a lot of traffic at the airport."

"Oh, no!" I told him. "Now he's gonna want one. And so will Dan."

"Well, he won't get the money from me to buy a Harley, Harriet. Or a Vespa, either. I'm the tightwad, you're the generous one." Jules said this lightheartedly but it felt like the truth, and my fault, especially since Dan had told me as much himself.

Lydia's face was impassive, but her eyes were darting from my face to Jules' face. I remembered then, she had done some acting and directing in addition to writing. Jules too had done his share of acting lessons when he was thinking about directing. That's something I thought about later, how the two of them had skills in that area.

Beautiful, fresh from her shower, Lydia went for the plate of muffins and bit into one declaring it "a masterpiece." In fact quite the most delicious healthy thing she'd ever eaten and was I going to make them for my show?

"Here, Jules," she said, "have one of Harriet's magnificent muffins." She handed him one and he took it. From her bare hand. And popped a big hunk of it in his mouth. That in itself was the deadest giveaway yet. *He ate food from her unwashed hand.* But I only thought about that later because just then, the phone rang. Arianna was calling to say she was probably going to be late as she and Bob had just had a fight and Bob had stormed out of the house and knowing him, he wouldn't be back for hours and hours.

Arianna's always late because of one reason or another and always holds up whatever feast we're having whether it's Passover or Thanksgiving or just a dinner party. So I went from being pissed at Jules for the motorcycle to pissed at Arianna for being late hours in advance.

By now it was close to ten thirty. Valentina and her family arrived. Jules set off for the airport. I'd forgotten how handsome Jesus is. Handsome and dignified, though he's very young like Valentina, not even thirty. He always shakes my hand with his rough one in the most endearing way, letting me know how happy he is that I love his wife and she loves me.

I sent Jesus to watch the game on TV and Lydia introduced herself to Angel, whom I hadn't seen in months and months. He had grown at least six inches and had that sort of loping walk boys get when they're growing too fast, like ponies. Valentina and I set to work. At noon, darling Sam burst in the door with his backpack and Lydia's unwashed hand-feeding of Jules was temporarily forgotten.

I wonder if I'll ever see any of those guests again who came to Thanksgiving. Our neighbors Boyd and Gary, who are the funniest couple I know, and who were in the process of developing a baby with the help of a surrogate in Tennessee. We're Facebook friends but that's not the same as getting to hold their baby. And that makes me sad.

Margaret and Tom were there too, my Southern old-people friends who I always invited to family events and for whom I took out the damask napkins and the silverware that belonged to my grandmother. It's good to have elders at family events and use one's fancy stuff, even if it's more labor intensive. We were distinctly lacking in the elder department.

Arianna and Bob arrived and it was clear they were still not speaking to one another. Arianna and Sam immediately disappeared out the back door, and I knew that meant one thing and one thing only: marijuana, plus tobacco.

By now it was four o'clock. Everybody except Jules and Jesus had drunk a glass of wine. The two of them shared a beer. I don't do nibbles on Thanksgiving because it's just too much. We all sat down in the dining room we almost never use.

Lydia reappeared with Angel and she went for the wine bottle. I could tell by the shy smile on Angel's face that the first tutoring session had gone well.

Freeman, as I expected, did show up. And he showed up alone, after everybody had already sat down, and brought with him two magnums of Dom. Freeman is far worse than Arianna, though I was pissed at her for aiding and abetting Sam's pot smoking. Or maybe Sam was aiding and abetting her pot smoking. Though I never get pissed at Sam.

Freeman made a point of squeezing in right next to Lydia, who made a point of making room for him. Valentina and I gave everybody a champagne flute. Freeman cracked out the Dom and then the table really started getting tipsy, everyone but Jules, who isn't much of a drinker. He was glowering from the head of the table at his brother, who was pouring out the bubbly and chatting up our pretty houseguest. But I saw Lydia hand him a corn muffin—using the silver tongs this time—then handing him the butter, and my husband cheering right up. Probably they were playing footsies under the table. Probably they were doing tons of revealing stuff that everybody else picked up on.

Although even I was aware that Jules didn't like sharing Lydia with Freeman. But I was used to their sibling rivalry and didn't dwell on it then.

Sam sat right next to me and kept everyone at the table amused just by being Sam. Sam's wonderfully charming, high or not.

As I have mentioned Thanksgiving is my very favorite holiday, but it's a lot of work. I had wine on an empty stomach (all that tasting kills the appetite) and then champagne, and then immediately went on drunk autopilot. The four different warnings I received went right over my head as they were being administered. It was only later that the cumulative effect of them hit me in the face like a whipped cream pie, showing me what a fool I was.

First Boyd came in the kitchen; I was reheating the gravy for second helpings, whisking it in my favorite little copper pot. Boyd's face was red. He too was tipsy. "Harriet," he said, "who's the girl?"

"What girl?"

"The lovely limey with the big boobs."

"She's my friend," I replied.

"Did she really say she was living here?"

"Yes," I replied.

Boyd stared at me like he had never seen me before. "Okay, honey!" Then he kissed me.

Arianna, who always brings a pie and ice cream, was next. "Harriet, I haven't seen you in a while. What's going on over here? Who is that girl with the English accent? She told me she's staying in Dan's room. Is that true?"

"Yes," I replied.

"Who is she?"

"My friend."

We were trying to get the gelato a little softer. I was at the sink with the ice cream scooper, running hot water over it.

"I wouldn't have her in my house."

"Why? She's talented and beautiful and very charming. She's a pleasure to have around."

"Oh my God, Harriet. I'm totally sick of Bob, but it's not like I want him to go anywhere."

"Jules isn't going anywhere, Arianna." And of course I was telling the truth, Jules didn't go anywhere; it was little old me who was in the process of being replaced and ousted.

Even Margaret, the most tactful Southern lady I know, managed to get me alone before the end of the evening. "Harriet, my dear, let's have lunch sometime soon; remember, I'm always just around the corner if you need me. You're as dear to me as a daughter." And she hugged me, bringing with her a whiff of Chanel and moth-balls from her silk dress.

Clearly everyone was aware that an English bombshell was exploding in my house.

But it wasn't until everybody but Freeman had gone home, all the dishes were done, the extra leaves in the table taken out, and the crystal put away, that the news even registered. By then, I was too tired to be really aware that the bomb had already detonated, as it were.

The three of them—Freeman, Lydia, and Jules—were in the living room, watching a movie. Sam and I were in the kitchen. Then and only then did I actually hear the warning that had been on everyone's lips.

He was eating his after-Thanksgiving sandwich and we were playing gin. Something we have been doing since I taught him to play when he was four.

I said to my son what I say every year. "I always wonder at the end of Thanksgiving why I went to so much trouble."

Sam smiled and took a bite. "For the sandwich, how come you're not having turkey this year? It's the best turkey sandwich. Have some turkey, Harriet!"

"I'm giving up eating birds too. It's hypocritical."

"Gin!" declared Sam. "Eleven-card gin."

I threw in my hand. "When you were little I always let you win a few hands, so you wouldn't get discouraged. But now I can't win to save my life. Pretty soon you'll start letting me win because you feel sorry for me."

Sam shuffled and dealt. "Dad seems mellow," he said and I could tell that pleased him. "I think the Harley cheers him up."

"I hate that thing."

"I know you must be upset about your dog, but still you should go out on it with him."

I nodded.

"I wish you could have met Marco."

"Hey, I always wanted a dog," Sam reminded me. Of course that made me feel just awful, but Sam wasn't interested in making me feel guilty about his lack of a dog. "Too bad Jules didn't have a bike when we were growing up. He might not have been so pissed off all the time. In fact, I've never seen him so happy."

We kept on playing. My hand was looking pretty good. Three aces, a pair of Jacks, and a run of hearts.

Sam was right, Jules had never seemed better. And for the first time in our marriage, he was arriving home at reasonable hours. Was it the salubrious effect of riding the dangerous LA freeways on a death machine? Or was the warm glow that came off him due to the Lydia Effect?

"What's with the English girl in Dan's room? I'm glad you put her there and not in my room!"

"Your room's too messy for company."

"She ain't exactly OCD like Dan." Sam laughed. "Have you been in there?"

"Valentina complains that she's messy."

Sam was studying his hand. "What I don't get is why she's living with us. Whose idea was it? Yours or Dad's?"

"Mine, she needs a place to live."

Sam was studying his hand, rearranging a few cards. His voice sounded earnest and serious, not lighthearted and ironic as it usually was.

"Ma, you look great, but come on; she's practically my age. Did you see the way that douche bag Freeman was slobbering over her? It's not as if he ever has a girlfriend or anybody. Dan and I think he's a closet case. I think he just likes to razz Dad up."

"Did Jules seem razzed up?" I asked innocently.

Sam laid down a seven. I drew a Jack.

"Ha! Gin!" I put down my cards. "I finally beat you!"

Sam too laid down his cards. "I let you win."

Then, and only then, did it occur to me that having Lydia around wasn't such a great idea. And more to the point, how in the world was I going to get her out?

"Sam," I said, "I'm going upstairs to take a shower. And I'm probably gonna scream. Don't get scared."

"I won't. I remember."

"Good," I said. "There used to be some kind of therapy called Primal Scream, I think that's what it is. My throat hurts afterward, but I feel better."

"Hey, it's cool, Ma. You gonna tell the others?"

"Nah," I said. Your dad is used to me. He'll tell the others."

And so I went upstairs. It was still early, about nine thirty, but I felt like it was the middle of the night, given all the work I'd done that day. I let the hot water beat down on me, I shaved my legs, but I was too tired to scream.

Instead, I took a sleeping pill and went to bed.

Fifteen

It was our last weekend as the family we had been, minus Dan of course. Not that the three of us were together much. Not that Jules and I were together much. Though Jules asked me first, it was Lydia who ended up going on his motor-cycle. Not me. It was Lydia who ended up with a black leather jacket. Not me. She claimed she got it at a sale at such a deal, and simply couldn't resist. I think, however, that Jules probably bought it for her.

I was sitting at the kitchen table reading a book when the two of them came in, helmets in hand.

"Hi!" I said cheerfully. "You've been on the dread machine with Jules."

"Where's Sam?" Jules wanted to know. "I was going to take him out."

"He's out with friends."

Was Lydia just the tinniest bit self-conscious? I think so, because as I unabashedly studied her flushed cheeks, her long legs, her leather jacket, she turned away.

"Where shall I put the helmet, Jules?"

Jules held out his hand. "I'll put it away."

By now, I was dying for Jules. Dying like a sixteen year old, like an old maid, like I had in the days when we were first together. Dying for him so much, I felt shy from it.

And that evening I reached for him. Just as he had reached for me Thanksgiving morning. My legs were shaved, my hair was washed, and I tickled his balls a little, which used to be our signal in the old days.

Nothing doing. He feigned sleep. I lay there in the dark and feigned sleep as well. We stayed that way for a good while. I began to breathe deeply so he'd think I was off in the Ambien daze and wouldn't remember anything the next morning.

Presently, Jules sprang from the bed. I couldn't see what he was doing but I could guess. He was pulling on his sweatpants and fluffing his hair, then he turned when he got to the door to make his final check on sleeping Harriet.

I counted to three hundred then I tiptoed out into the hallway. There was a light on in Lydia's room. Was she in there? Was Jules in there with her?

Then I heard laughter coming from downstairs. Lydia's laughter, Jules laughter, and then Sam's infectious giggle. Of course! They were down in the kitchen hacking away at the turkey, having a great time.

There was some light on in the hallway from one of those ecologically sound low-wattage lightbulbs I insisted on using. The light they cast is so ugly. I looked down at myself, the fortysomething in good shape, Little Miss Eraser Chest with muscley arms. What a contrast I made to Lydia who was probably in something fetching with a cute little camisole top showing off those big, real twentysomething orbs of hers.

Be careful what you wish for, Harriet. Hadn't Lydia herself said this to me?

The next morning, Sam was standing with his backpack in the front hallway; the thing was so stuffed he seemed to be swaying from side to side.

"Be careful!" I cautioned him. "Hold on tight!"

Lydia floated down the stairs after he had gone.

"He's left, has he?"

"Yes," I said.

Lydia hugged me. Her long, warm arms comforted me. I didn't let myself think about how they wound themselves around Jules.

"He's a lovely boy, so bright and full of

promise. He reminds me of you. I so enjoyed getting to know him. We ate turkey sandwiches last night and got to know one another."

"Thank you. You're a good girl, too!" And she was a good girl in many ways. Ambition, lust, envy; these are not easy things to have to deal with, even for the strongest of characters. She wanted a start in life. And I had handed it to her on a silver platter.

That was Sunday morning. The day before we all went to a movie together at the Third Street Promenade, which was teeming with people on a holiday weekend, one of the biggest box office times of the year.

I wasn't paying attention and I lost them coming out of the movie. For ten long minutes I couldn't find them. I didn't want to text; that looked too desperate. And no one texted me. Which meant they weren't thinking of me. People were everywhere: families, sweethearts, people with dogs, panhandlers singing for dollar bills, even one of the first of the season's bell ringers for the Salvation Army was out. Everybody had someone but me. I knew then I had lost whatever I used to have. I wanted my family back; I wanted Jules back. Then, at last, Lydia found me. She smiled and said, "Harriet, we've been looking for you everywhere!" and I felt momentarily better. Then we all went home together.

That evening, just the three of us, Jules, Lydia, and I, were at home. I took a long, hot shower and imagined them kissing furtively—passionately—somewhere in the house. The thought of it made me furious but also turned me on. I imagined all sorts of things in the shower: twosomes with Lydia and me, threesomes with the three of us.

But mostly I just wanted Jules back the way it had been.

Knowing that wasn't going to happen, I let out one of my long bloodcurdling screams worthy of Janet Leigh in the shower with Anthony Perkins. In fact, it was my swan song, I never screamed there (or anyplace else) again. And I don't think I will. The era of the Primal Scream is over for me now that Jules and I are no longer together.

That evening, I imagined scaring the shit out of Lydia. At least she must have jumped. I wondered if someone would call the cops, or were my neighbors used to the howling by then.

I imagined Jules, who was used to all my carryings on, holding on to her ass, running those clever hands of his up her skirt, middle finger in the honey pot. "It's nothing! Just Harriet screaming. She always screams in the shower."

I had no choice but to leave them alone together on Monday morning when I left to do my show.

I was so sure of my material that I nailed it on the first take:

"There are two ways to mend a broken heart. Make-up sex and make-up dinner. If one doesn't work, try the other."

On the way home from the set, I shopped for ingredients. And when I got home, I started cooking. The house was empty. I was making lamb stew, Jules' old favorite, and something I hadn't given him for years since I gave up eating lamb myself.

When Valentina arrived, she joined me.

"You having company tonight, Harriet?"

"No. Just Jules, I haven't made him this for a long time. It has to sit for a while."

"What will you eat?"

"I haven't thought about that. There's always something in the freezer. And salad stuff."

"Lydia? She eat here every night?"

"No," I said. I was finished browning the lamb. Now it had to sit there for a while before I added the red wine, the vegetables, and lastly, the mushrooms. "Lydia told me she has a date tonight."

"She such a pretty girl, Harriet."

"Yes."

"A girl like that can have all the boyfriends she wants. Angel I think he have a crush on her."

"Good, then he'll listen to her."

"I shouldn't have said those mean things about her. Jesus say—"

But I didn't want to hear what Jesus said about Lydia. Or what a nice girl she was and how pretty.

"How about we make some biscuits. And don't forget to remind me to squeeze some juice. Orange, carrot, and also apple. It's always nice to have two or three kinds of juice in the fridge."

But Jules didn't come home that night to drink or eat. Not until pretty late. He was his usual contrite self.

"I'm so sorry, honey, I missed the lamb stew. You know how much I love lamb stew, but it will be better tomorrow. It's always better the next day."

Yes, Jules right up until the end was a great apologizer. He did it so well, it took me years to figure out his apologies were absolutely meaningless because everything he said he was sorry about always happened again sometime shortly thereafter. Again and again and again.

Instead of going to bed like a good girl, I was up watching the ten o'clock movie. One of the best movies ever.

I was crying as I watched *The Best Years of our Lives*. It was the scene where Wilma is helping her armless lover get into his pajama top. The two are so tender with one another. And there's so much love in the scene.

"I can't believe you're still up," Jules said and sat down beside me on the couch. "Fucking great movie! The guy without the arms kills me. You know he wasn't a pro. He really was a guy who lost his arms in the war. That's what makes it so great." Jules got up from the couch, turned to go.

"There's juice, Jules."

"Thanks, I'm just going to bed. I'm beat."

Fucked out? I wondered.

"Jules?"

"Yes?"

"It's fresh."

"What are you talking about?"

"Juice. I squeezed juice." I turned; Jules was standing in the doorway. "Lydia's not in yet," I said. "Maybe she had a hot date. What do you think?"

Jules was staring at the screen. By now the movie had progressed to that monumental scene with the field of empty war airplanes. "Great scene!" Jules sighed. "Fucking genius!"

"Will you take me for a ride on your bike?"

Jules' reply was very sweet. Jules' sweetness is deceptive because it sounds so sweet, like his apologies sound so sincere. I always thought he was sweet when he sounded like that. Yes, even that night with all I knew, he deceived me.

"That's okay, Harriet. You don't have to do anything so scary."

"And neither do you. In fact I think we should talk."

I couldn't see his face because the room was dark. Did he look scared?

"We need to talk," he said this lightly. "For a man, the four most dreaded words in any language."

"We need to talk though, Jules."

"About what?"

"Just don't," I begged him. Yes, I think I was begging him.

"Don't what?"

"Don't rock the lifeboat!"

Because I knew now the New Me was real, I knew they must have been together that evening. The next morning, when I came in from my run, I knocked on Lydia's door. I decided I had nothing to lose: I'd give it the old college try and ask her to leave.

I knocked again. Lydia wasn't answering. The door was open, and since it was still my house after all, I decided to just go in.

Dan's room had never been so messy. Clothes were strewn over chairs. The closet door open and all Lydia's paraphernalia was everywhere. The desk too was untidy, the laptop screen open. The bed of course was unmade, the pretty lavender quilt I had put there was balled up.

Then something moved and I screamed. It was Pasha who had hidden himself in Lydia's bedclothes. He stood on his four solid legs and gave me a reproachful look, then hopped down off the bed and left the room. Seeing Pasha on Lydia's bed like that made me realize I'd made the biggest mistake of my life.

"Traitor!" I would have loved to have clawed my faithless cat. First my dog, and now fraternizing with my enemy.

Then the front door shut. *Shit*, I thought, *I'm busted*.

Lydia bounded up the stairs.

"I don't mean to be trespassing. Pasha was meowing. I'm afraid you locked him in your room. He just left this second.

"Sometimes I think you've put a spell on him," I continued.

"Nonsense!"

"No really, what heart he has belongs to you."

"Well the feeling is mutual, Harriet."

I noticed then that Lydia had on running clothes. "I didn't know you ran."

"Your discipline is inspiring. I'm just following your example. Especially with all this eating going on."

"I didn't see you out there. I ran around the

country club and down to the ocean. How about you?"

"Just the streets. By the way, I'm off to see Freeman this afternoon. We're going to have a meeting about my script and my career. He's going to start introducing me around."

I was happy for her. I couldn't help it, I really was. The career part. Not the Jules part, however-er.

"You're wonderful, Harriet. None of this would have happened but for your incredible generosity. I'll never forget what you've done for me."

"It's easy for me to be generous. Holding on has always been my problem."

And then she said it, I swear on a stack of bibles she said, "Keep holding on, Harriet."

I looked her right in the face, wanting to see her eyes. "You mean that?"

"Yes," she said evenly.

"Are we talking about the same thing?"

"Yes, I'm looking at apartments. I'll be out of here soon and out of your life. You have nothing to scream about. Just give me a little time to find a place to live."

"Ah," I said, "so, you heard me?"

"In more ways than one."

Smart girl, I thought, "Of course," I said to her, "of course take some time."

Yes, there was closeness, a sense of affection

even then. We had something between us besides Jules.

"Not to mention what poor Pasha will do without you."

"And I'll miss you as well!" Her eyes were lowered when she said this; I was guessing she felt sad or maybe ashamed. I felt a little ashamed for kicking her out.

Since she had made it so easy for me by volunteering to leave, I was determined to be a lady, as my friend Margaret would say. I walked over to her. She was standing by the windows with the morning light pouring off her hair, her young skin, her long legs and arms. I thought a hug was overdoing it. Instead I extended my hand. She raised her eyes and looked at me resolutely as she shook my hand firmly.

Then I left the room, thinking I had dodged the bullet.

Sixteen

THE CALM AFTER THE STORM, OR SO I THOUGHT. I DIDN'T let myself obsess about them anymore. As far as I was concerned they would play it out, and then it would be over. The end of the affair as they say.

Lydia was scurrying around with printouts from West Side Rental. When she was home, she was at her computer looking things up on Craigslist.

Jules was keeping normal hours, coming home for dinner, leaving by 8:00 in the morning and home by 8:00 too, the first time in our marriage he was present with any kind of regularity.

In a way it was a good time. We were all super polite to one another. Jules and Lydia hardly made eye contact. There was none of the tension of Thanksgiving weekend—it was as it had been when she first moved in. We were the perfect modern family. I caught myself more than once thinking, *She should just stay.* Jules was in a great mood, Lydia didn't have the wolf at the door—as long as I didn't have to accept a ménage à trios, with them disappearing into their own room, I was okay.

No, I never did catch Jules and Lydia with the bed creaking in Dan's room.

No, the bed creaking in Dan's room had actually happened about a year ago, but it was Sam and his then-girlfriend, Katie. Not Jules and Lydia. Shocking nonetheless. I only asked Sam one question—why didn't he use his own room? Sam gave me one of his 'Are you nuts, Harriet' looks and replied, "If you were a girl, wouldn't you rather do it in Dan's room, not mine?"

Then, one night, Jules didn't come home and neither did Lydia. I told myself not to stress, it was all going to be okay, and I went to bed with a book and fell asleep without a pill. Of course I woke up. I was alone in my empty bed. I looked over and it was 3:07 by the bedside digital clock. I reached for my phone and texted him: "R U OK?" He didn't text back.

Then I lay down in the dark and presently heard the Harley roar into the driveway. Jules was okay. His cheating ass was alive. He came up the stairs and tiptoed around our room. Not too long after, he slid into bed.

I didn't say anything. My rationale was, *Of*

course they've got to say goodbye. There may be a couple more of these late nightmares and then it will be over. Lydia and I had shaken hands. We'd made a deal, and I believed in that deal. I guess I had to believe in something.

Before long I heard another key rattle in the lock downstairs. This time it was Lydia. I imagined her whispering, "Pasha, Pasha I'm home!" just like I was in the habit of doing. She had taken up running, and she had taken up Pasha long before that. I could see her picking up his beautiful, heavy body, feeding him bits of something tasty, and then carrying him up to her messy bedroom.

It's winding down. It has to run its course. Best to just be silent and observe.

A couple of days went by. Maybe a week even.

We started having a string of Santa Anas when the days were bright, hot, and dusty—and the winds blew from the east. The winds kicked up at night and made the palm trees sing and the windows rattle. My hair was electric and my skin felt like a pachyderm. There were hundreds of new lines on my face it seemed.

I was in our tiny little backyard one early afternoon with a hat on, watering the herbs, when Valentina came out the side door and toward the back loaded down with clear plastic garbage bags. In her mouth she was clenching a bag full of recycling jars. Under her arms were newspapers.

I looked up from my watering, exasperated. During a Santa Ana everything is exasperating. Then I put the hose down and headed toward her.

Valentina's biggest fault is her insistence on taking one trip, when she should certainly be taking three or four. I can't rid her of this dangerous habit. She fell down the stairs last year when she was carrying the vacuum, the mop, and a bucket full of cleaning supplies. I don't know why an otherwise intelligent person would put herself at such peril, but she can't seem to control herself.

She had the strangest look on her face. One I'd never seen before. Then it hit me: she's angry. She's absolutely furious; smoke could be coming out of her nostrils. I tried to take away the clear plastic bag of our junk from her, but she clung to it. I thought, as I often do, *Where the fuck is all this trash coming from?* What were we throwing away for God's sake?

I could see a big blue box of tampons, mine actually. Eight zillion wads of toilet paper—Jules is always wadding up toilet paper for nose blowing, for holding things he considers unclean, the list goes on and on. Like paper towels, we went through literally cases of the stuff, the way a family of ten small children with the runs would go through it, even with the boys gone. Through the clear plastic I could see there was a home pregnancy kit among all the toilet paper and dental floss.

Like Twain said, "Denial ain't just a river in Africa." I concluded it was Valentina's home pregnancy kit and that's why she was pissed off. I decided on the spot she'd gone into Lydia's bathroom and given herself a pregnancy test, because at my house, of course, there was much more privacy than at the casa with Jesus and Angel and the extended family. There it was staring me in the face, but like a dope I was thinking, *Valentina won't get an abortion, how in the world are they going to feed another mouth over there. I better get to work so I can give her a raise.*

I held up the bag.

"All this garbage we produce every day. We've got to start composting too. January first, we're composting all our fruit and vegetable waste. Deal?"

Valentina nodded grimly. She was still pissed.

"You took the home pregnancy test. Are you pregnant?"

"No, Harriet."

"You sure?"

"Yes, Harriet."

"You wouldn't hide that from me, would you, I'd always help you."

"I know that, Harriet."

"You were cleaning Lydia's room?"

Valentina gestured to me that she had.

"She's sort of messy, like Sam, isn't she? Maybe we should have put her in Sam's room." This made Valentina smile. "But we'll forgive her because she's helping Angel, right?"

"Yes," said Valentina. There was something distinctly strange about that yes.

"She's leaving soon anyway; everybody is coming home for Christmas. Dan's bringing Indira. He's giving her his room and sleeping on the living room couch because she's a very proper girl from a good family and she would be uncomfortable sharing his room in front of us."

Valentina smiled, her good humor was coming back.

I was babbling because I was nervous. Afraid of the silence. Is that why Jules always talked and talked and talked? Did quiet and being inside his own head give him the willies? For the future it was certainly something to think about.

"Lydia's looking for apartments right this minute. She told me this morning. Hey, I made you one of those energy drinks. It's in the fridge."

"I drink it already."

Seventeen

THAT AFTERNOON, I WENT TO A HARLEY DAVIDSON dealership in Venice and talked the guy into giving me a ride around the neighborhood. He wasn't supposed to. I had gone there thinking I would learn how to ride a motorcycle and surprise Jules—maybe I'd like it and we could get his and her Harley's—a sure way to turn the boys off any cachet associated with motorcycles.

"What if I want to buy one?" I asked.

"You have to take a safety course and pass a test before you get your license."

"Will you show me how to turn it on? The key thing? How to do the gas?"

The guy laughed. He was very nice actually. He showed me and it wasn't that hard; I'm pretty good with my hands.

He took me for the forbidden spin around the block, and the second we got going I knew I could never drive such a thing. Or do what I was doing now, holding on for dear life. I was giddy with fright the whole time and kept my eyes squeezed shut. One glimpse of the world whirling by so terrifyingly was enough for me.

The next day was Saturday. I'd gone to the Saturday market very early. By late morning, I was at the stove with all six burners going. Lydia was at the old oak table at her laptop, pecking away contentedly. We were on our best behavior, like it was the first days of our friendship and none of the stuff with Jules had gone down. She was so pretty and her English accent so charming.

"It smells divine, Harriet. What are you creating today?"

She was flattering me. And of course, I was flattered. All cooks like to think they are creative artists.

"We're having lots of different vegetables, millet, and corn bread. I'm toasting the millet before I add the mushrooms, which I've already sautéed with garlic in butter. Millet tastes like mush unless you roast it beforehand. I like to roast it dry, because it comes out nuttier than when you roast it in oil or butter."

"So much to remember!"

"It's second nature after a while. Like writing, I'm guessing. Oh and I'm making some dead animal for you and Jules."

Lydia was very cheerful. "I thought I smelled

a savory smell! Goodie! What kind of dead animal?"

"Chicken."

"Yay! I love your chicken."

We fell silent for a while. Lydia at her laptop, me at the stove with my back turned.

Lydia said, "If I didn't eat meat, I wouldn't be as generous as you. I'd let us bring it in from the outside."

"You're braver than I am. And less eager to please. Maybe that's a good thing."

Just then Jules arrived. I turned around to see him carrying in his dry cleaning. I was remembering too, during Marco's very brief reign, how he'd yip and bark excitedly when Jules came in the door. He had absolutely adored Jules.

"We have to switch dry cleaners," my husband announced cheerfully. Too many women in sports utility vehicles in the parking lot. Too bad you can't carry dry cleaning on a bike . . ."

Lydia laughed.

Yes, even Jules' complaining wasn't angry anymore. He seemed funny, not a middle-aged kvetch with a chip on his shoulder.

Precise as always, I heard from behind me the sound of Jules putting his keys on the hook next to the back door. Then he washed his hands in the laundry room sink. He washed and he washed. Then the familiar sound of the paper towel roll, *thrump, thrump, thrump*, dispensing at least seventy-five cents worth every quarter hour.

"Do I smell lunch?" he called out.

"Five minutes."

The Santa Ana was over, thank God. The fog had started rolling in the evening before. And it was chilly. People never think of Southern California as being chilly but it is. The evenings, the early mornings. Here it was midday and I was happy I had made hot food. We needed it.

Or maybe I just needed to make food.

Jules disappeared upstairs. Lydia excused herself and went to put her laptop away. But they both came right back down and took their places at the table.

I had drooping fronds of rosemary in three vanilla bottles on the table because there wasn't anything much growing in the garden now. Their spicy scent filled the room. The nasturtiums I loved in salads were over but the Japanese persimmons were at the market. I had a bowl of them sliced with walnuts, a little oil, and pomegranate seeds. I had cheated and bought pomegranate seeds already peeled, a tiny little thing of them cost eight dollars. Jules didn't like pomegranates, claiming they got stuck in his teeth, but I knew Lydia loved them, and I certainly did.

I filled a plate with the millet, the kale, the roasted peppers decorated with purple basil, and a chicken breast—Lydia liked white meat—and set it down in front of her. She smiled and looked grateful. I did the same for Jules, giving him the leg because he likes dark meat, and he too looked happy. Though I was thinking that Jules never seemed very grateful, I guess he was so used to being fed and catered to that he didn't know enough to be grateful.

Yes, Jules seemed as happy as I'd ever seen him. Sam had remarked on it. Certainly happier than he ever was when it was just our family: the boys and me. As long as he had to play Mommy and Daddy there was always something to complain about. Children—certainly strong-willed, intelligent males like ours—needed to assert themselves. How else would they learn how to negotiate outside the home? But only one male was allowed to assert himself at our house.

Which was why our triangle was much more to his liking than an everyday normal family life with all its tensions and competition. I'd gotten myself into this fix to begin with, I think, to get a little help with Jules, to take a load off as they say. I don't know if I saw that then, or only now when I'm remembering.

In spite of all this, I was greatly looking forward to having my house back and my husband too. Lydia knew that Indira was coming for

Christmas and would be in "her" room. I'd keep it the way it was with the new quilt and pillows for Dan's girlfriend. Then it would double as a guest room.

Gloria would come in the spring as she always did, in that dead time when there was nothing much at the market before the summer stuff appeared and she'd always remark that she didn't understand why everybody made such a fuss about the fruit and vegetables in Southern California, and couldn't we all just order in a pizza and eat Chinese food? Yes, that day thinking of returning to the status quo, even if it involved Jules' mother's annual visit, was the one thing that kept me from losing it completely. What I kept saying to myself was we have to get through these days as pleasantly as possible. Which of course seems totally contradictory, but who said life is always on the nose?

Jules had two helpings of chicken and then finally pushed his plate a little away. "I'm stuffed," he said.

"Me too! I'm running as soon as I digest all this delicious lunch," Lydia said.

Jules burped. It was a polite sort of burp, not the kind he often let loose when it was just the two of us alone. A burp or a fart. He excused himself elaborately.

Just for the record, only once did I accidently fart in front of Jules in all those years together.

And he was shocked and appalled and chided me with righteous indignation. I think that sort of sums up the true nature of our relationship.

Jules sighed presently. "Lucullus has dined with Lucullus," he declared, this was a reference to some horrible Roman emperor who set a fine table, and was Jules' highest praise next to a seat on the lifeboat. Apparently his father used to say that during his brief tenure in Jules' life. Jules, not that I can recall, ever said simply, "thank you, that was wonderful, I can't believe you make me dinner every night," just, "Lucullus has dined with Lucullus." I bet the empress and all the senators in ancient Rome got sick of hearing that too. Never mind the servants who actually made and served the food.

Then Jules laid his hands across his belly that was sticking out just a bit from the big meal and he looked at us both and he smiled contentedly, yes, even a little smugly.

I saw Lydia studying his face and a dark look passed over her own. After meals was one of Jules' satisfied times, after sex too. It was clear that she didn't like this contented mood that had spread over the table like soft butter on bread.

She sprang to her feet.

"Harriet," she announced briskly, "you sit. Do you want tea or coffee?"

Jules grabbed the newspaper from the chair

where I had laid it and began perusing the head-lines.

"Tea, please. Some of the Assam. And I'd like it with honey. You know where the honey is, don't you?"

Lydia made me tea. I sat contently, and when she placed it down in front of me with the pot of honey, I smiled up at her.

Then she sat down.

She was wearing a tight blue top that made her incredible boobs even more incredible. Her straight black hair shined. Her thick eyebrows gave her the look of a high-fashion model. She was gorgeous, twentysomething, and talented. It was obvious she was pissed off at this fortysomething husband of mine, sitting there so smugly reading the newspaper. I wonder if she had checked out any of his other adorable habits, like the paper goods we went through every month. His having to have his way all the time. His temper . . .

"I'm going to visit friends in Sonoma next week. That way, Dan can have his room back. I'll hurry up and make sure everything is in order, spit spot."

"You sound just like Mary Poppins!"

"I was doing it on purpose. I know you love Mary Poppins, all Americans do."

Was there just a hint of derision, in the "all Americans do?" I think there was. They look down on us, I think, the way we look up to them. At least it seems that way to me.

"I never liked it that she left when the wind changed. We used to have to turn off the video player when Dan was little. He could never watch Mary Poppins without crying his eyes out."

Jules either put the newspaper down or looked over it, I can't remember which. "I don't remember that," he said.

"You weren't usually around during video watching time."

"Now, now, Harriet."

"I wasn't being critical, just stating the facts."

"I know I wasn't around a lot," he said sweetly. It sounded like he regretted it. But Jules always was so good at sounding regretful. And who knows, maybe he was regretful.

"It's okay, Jules, it's all over and done with."

I looked at Jules and this time it wasn't a fake. Lucullus might have dined with Lucullus, but now the wolf was at the door and Jules looked absolutely stricken. I realize he too must have been in denial. He thought he was going to be getting away with this forever. Like Valentina always said, "He only thinking about Jules!"

"What are you talking about? Nothing is over and done with!"

I caught the look on Lydia's face then. It

wasn't pretty.

I keep coming back to the fact that she trained in theater. Her timing was perfect. Calmly and with precision, she announced, "Jules, you know what she's talking about. Harriet knows." Then she looked at me. "Don't you Harriet?"

I don't think all that well on my feet, though of course I was sitting down. I can be cute on the set and funny when there's not too much at stake. But that afternoon in December I was plenty nervous. And shocked. Because it was happening; I was hearing the words I was hoping with all my heart not to hear.

I swallowed and my throat felt like a golf ball was wedged there.

I gulped. "I guess I've known all along."

Jules too looked shocked. His ears were lying back. I thought of Marco, whose ears had lain back when he heard a noise that scared him. I had a wild urge to go over and pat his silky curls and say, "There, there, Jules."

"No! Please!" said my husband. "I didn't mean for it to happen this way!"

Lydia forged on. By then Jules had his head on the table.

"I realize there are moral consequences to pay for doing this. But I'm prepared to pay. I've made up my mind."

I was on my feet finally. I couldn't just sit

there.

"We had a deal. We shook hands. What about Freeman, what about how you said you were grateful?"

How cold she seemed suddenly.

"Maybe I want it all, Harriet. I never said I was generous like you, did I?"

"But I thought you were honorable."

"Not always."

We all sat silently. I felt like we were in some kind of a play. My direction was to get up and walk around the room, nonplussed. Jules' was to raise his head timidly and to look from one woman to the other. The nonstop yapper was rendered silent by the women.

It was Lydia's turn to explain. "You introduced me to Jules. You got him to help me with my script. You brought me in here. It was almost as if you wanted all this to happen. And now that it has you've changed your mind."

"There's no law against changing your mind. People change their minds all the time."

"I changed my mind too, Harriet. It's too late; Jules and I are staying together."

"You're what?"

"We're in love."

"You hardly know him. He hardly knows you."

For a creative writer, Lydia was ridden with clichés. She'll probably do really well in the film business. I'm being catty perhaps. When people are in love they don't choose their language all that carefully. And when you're in love everything feels new.

"Yes," she said, "everything happened so fast. But love's like that. We want a family!"

Then, of course, I put it together. The right way this time with the home pregnancy test. Valentina was furious because she knew what it meant.

I looked at Jules.

"Jules, do you love her?"

He nodded sheepishly.

"But you love me too. I know you do."

Once again Jules nodded and his nod conveyed how very sorry he was. Yes, he was the consummate apologizer.

"So who is it going to be in your lifeboat? Lydia or me? You can't have us both anymore."

We both looked at Jules who looked just plain scared.

Finally, I announced, "I'd like to speak to Jules alone."

I am forty-four, she's twenty-eight, and this was LA, not exactly a country where the mature female is regarded as a sex object. Actually, in a few years Lydia would be over the hill herself, and maybe she knew this.

But in the meantime, my rival had no problem leaving me alone with Jules.

"Of course! I'll go up and start packing."

At least she'll be gone, I thought, still in denial, thinking Jules would stay here with me. At least we all don't have to live under one roof anymore. I heard her go up the stairs. Was Pasha waiting for her on the bed?

Jules' eyes were cast down at the newspaper.

"Would it kill you to make some eye contact?"

But Jules couldn't face me. He was actually reading the newspaper just like it was any ordinary day when he was ignoring me.

"Are you really going to read this newspaper?"

"I'm nervous. It relaxes me."

I should have said, "Fine! Be that way," and told him to go relax at a motel with Lydia for the rest of his life.

I didn't. I made a pitch.

"Do you really want to do this? We've been together almost half our lives. What about the boys? Are you going to tell them?"

"They've got their own stuff going on. They'll deal with it. I dealt with it myself with Gloria—I didn't feel a thing."

"Freeman didn't feel anything either, huh? I guess that's why you two can't imagine anyone else feels anything."

"Freeman's got nothing to do with this. I keep telling Lydia he's a jerk and a suit and probably is just stringing her along."

"I disagree. I think you're competing with Freeman as usual."

That was something Jules didn't want to hear. He got up. Then he too went upstairs. I guess it was then I realized he wasn't staying. And I was totally shocked!

Nineteen years of marriage! The twins! All the food I made at all hours! And that was it?

Apparently so.

I picked up the platter of fruit. I had a great urge to hurl it against the wall. Had I been younger, I might have. But I had learned a little about controlling myself lately. Besides, it was my favorite platter, an old Spode earthenware without any chips, a wedding present from a friend of my mother. Why should I destroy something I valued? Hadn't I done enough of that sort of thing?

I went to the fridge and took out the pitcher of fresh carrot juice. Then passed through the laundry room and grabbed Jules' keys. I knew how to unlock the gas cap of the Harley.

It gave me great pleasure to imagine Jules' face when he found out. And to think of the sound of the Harley sputtering, then dying, perhaps orange colored liquid vomiting out.

How long would it take for him to figure out what had happened? Or would I tell him and watch his face as he went completely nuts? It was just a stupid flashy piece of equipment. And furthermore, he'd certainly be getting off easy after killing my dog and running off with my friend.

However, being Healthy Harriet and a sensible person (one who had stupidly signed a prenup back when I was a child), I didn't do anything like that. After I watched Jules and Lydia out the window, putting their suitcases in the back of the Beemer, I cried and cried all weekend and wished I never met her or made the New Me happen.

Three

months

later . . .

AFTER ALL IS SAID AND DONE, I REALIZE YES, I HAD A rather large hand in what went down at my house. If I didn't actually set out with firm intent to put the New Me in place, if I hadn't asked Lydia to move in with us, I guarantee I'd still be there screaming in the shower.

The real question remains: if I had to do the whole thing over again, would I? Part of me says yes, because I am, if not bursting with joy, much more steady than I've ever been. Steadiness is not a quality I would have ever regarded so highly, still now that I have it (relatively) it is like good air and fresh food: necessary. I like living alone, even in the cottage cheese plate; not worrying about who likes string beans and who hates eggplant. I ran two shifts of dinner for so many years in addition to my other work; I'm surprised I can still muster up any enthusiasm. But I love food. And cooking for people. A lot of what went wrong at my house was, I think, disguised by the food thing. Ultimately, it was the only way I had to express my love. Next time, I'm not going to make such a meager show of what I have to offer. Or maybe by then I'll have, as they say, more on my plate.

One last thing, I paid one more visit to my house at night. I told Valentina all about it when we met for lunch today.

We met, naturally, at a health food restaurant. Valentina looks great, and the woman she's working for now is giving her double what I did, and I paid her well. It pleases me to know I fixed up that wonderful paycheck for her. When her new boss asked me what I paid Valentina, I simply doubled it. She didn't turn a hair.

We were drinking our juices (carrot, beet, celery, and a bit of ginger) and she was describing her new circumstances.

"She say if I stay there, she'll pay my health insurance. They very, very rich. She scared all the time I'm leaving them. She love the way I cook. The little girl she love me so much!"

"Of course they love you. She's so lucky to have you. I wish I could take you all to New

York with me. Promise you won't forget me. We'll talk on the phone, we'll Skype."

"Angel, he doing that with the new computer you bought us."

"How's Angel?"

"Pretty good. You tell Dan and Sam I say hello?"

"Of course! Sam doesn't even seem to mind that I'm moving to New York. He says he'll come have dinner with me. I'm thrilled! And I'll be much closer to Dan. I'm so grateful I have that job to go to. Imagine! I'll be out of the kitchen. Jules' mother even called and said I could stay at her apartment while I'm getting settled if I wanted to. No more up at four thirty for *Healthy Harriet*. In fact, the last show runs this week!"

"I'm so happy for you, Harriet!"

"I'm thinking about going back to school when I get settled in. You're very smart and I want you to start thinking about it too. You don't have to be a housekeeper forever. You always said you wanted to be a nurse. You'd be a great nurse."

"I wish you let Jesus drive you to the airport. I make him clean out the truck. Why you no want him to? He want to."

We ate, we drank, we dipped our baked sweet potato sticks in the special ketchup without any corn syrup.

"Is she . . ."

Valentina knew just what I meant.

"She still helping Angel. They talking over the computer. She help him twice a week."

"Skype! They're Skyping. I sort of thought she wouldn't leave Angel behind."

Then I told my friend how I'd walked by there the other night. And it wasn't the first time.

"No one see you?"

"No, she didn't."

I could tell Valentina was studying my face, wondering if I knew. It was only three months since I moved out of there and Lydia was quite noticeably pregnant. That's what I saw when she stood up. And that's why I went back, to see if my eyes were deceiving me. They weren't.

Which meant they'd been carrying on all along! Maybe there was no New Me. Only the Old Me to be gotten rid of.

Still, I had, if not revenge, certainly closure.

The second night I went there to verify what I'd seen, the narrow window that faces the side of the house was open. I heard the landline ring. Jules is old-fashioned like I am. He always calls on the landline, not like the newer generation. We fortysomethingers think a real conversation is one carried out over a landline.

I was outside under the tree staring in. She got up from the cluttered table to run for the wall phone.

I of course didn't hear what was being said on the other end, but it was clearly Jules. I didn't have to approach the window to hear the, "Running late, are you?" or the, "But darling, you promised."

I was staring at Lydia's belly and the bigger-than-ever boobs. Don't get so upset, I felt like telling her, it's bad for the baby. If you don't react, maybe he'll have to learn some new tricks. Maybe he gets off on all this attention focused on him getting home. Don't make him so freaking important. In the meantime chill out! The last thing you want is all that stress hormone stuff churning around in the bloodstream.

I watched her hang up the phone. Then stand there for a moment: a pissed off Madonna.

And then came my reward: her bloodcurdling scream.

"Did I scream like that? As though the village was going to be sacked and all the babies speared by the Cossacks?"

Probably I did. We were quite a bit alike, as I always said.

Although I knew Valentina didn't know who the Cossacks were, she was enjoying my recitation, she got the point. She was laughing and rocking in her chair, clapping her hands in the way she does.

"Valentina, I wonder what the neighbors

think is going on with all these women screaming in there all the time? You remember how I
screamed?"

Valentina smiled.

The check came, and we both had to go. So I
didn't tell her the rest. How I turned and walked
away. But soon I was breaking out into a run. I
ran and I ran under a half moon with palm trees
against the sky, past the basketball hoops and
the sprinkler systems and the lit windows of my
old neighborhood to my car. Or, how running
free like that at night, away from all that would
never be mine again felt pretty damn good. Fabulous in fact. And how once I reached the car,
I leaned against the door, catching my breath,
happy to have gotten away.

Instead, I told her Jesus could drive me to the
airport. And that I was giving them the Volvo.

About the
Author

Mary Marcus was born and raised in Louisiana but left for New York after graduating from Tulane. She worked for many years in the advertising and fashion industries for Neiman Marcus, *Vogue*, Lancôme, Faberge, and San Rio Toys where she worked on the Hello Kitty brand. Marcus' short fiction has appeared in *North Atlantic Review*, *Karamu*, *Fiction*, *Jewish Women's Literary Journal* and *The New Delta Review* among others. She lives in Los Angeles and the East End of Long Island.